DO ME A FAVOR

FAVOR

AND

OTHER SHORT STORIES

°°

°°

ANNE PAOLUCCI

Library of Congress Cataloging-in-Publication Data

Paolucci, Anne.
  Do me a favor and other short stories / by Anne Paolucci.
    p. cm.
  Contents. A tape for Bronko – Do me a favor – Play it again! –
Half a story, a third of the pie – Kaleidoscope – Layover – Summer
solstice – Soho revisited – "If I should wake . . . ." – Mr. Gold.
  ISBN 0-918680-92-1 (alk. Paper)
    I. Title: Do me a favor. II. Title.

PS3566.A595 D6 2001
813',54–dc21

                                                        00-054862

oooooooooooooooooooooooooooooooooooooooooooooooooooooooooooooooooooooooooooooooooooooooo

Published for
THE BAGEHOT COUNCIL
by GRIFFON HOUSE PUBLICATIONS
P. O. Box 468
Smyrna DE 19977

CONTENTS

Other Works by the Same Author

°°

FICTION

• *EIGHT SHORT STORIES* (Introduction by Harry T. Moore) •
H. Prim Co., NJ (1977)
• *SEPIA TONES* •
1ˢᵗ Ed. Outrigger Publishers, New Zealand (1985)
2ⁿᵈ Ed. Griffon House Publications, NY (1986)
• *TERMINAL DEGREES* (A Novella) •
Potpourri Publications Co., KS (1997)

POETRY

• *POEMS WRITTEN FOR SBEK'S MUMMIES, MARIE MENKEN, AND
OTHER IMPORTANT PERSONS, PLACES & THINGS*
(Introduction by Glauco Cambon)) •
H. Prim Co., NJ (1977)
• *RIDING THE MAST WHERE IT SWINGS* •
Griffon House Publications, NY (1980)
• *GORBACHEV IN CONCERT (AND OTHER POEMS)* •
(Preface by Diana Der-Hovanessian)
Griffon House Publications, NY (1991)
• *QUEENSBORO BRIDGE (AND OTHER POEMS)* •
(Introduction by Nishan Parlakian)
Potpourri Publications Co., KS (1995)

PLAYS

• *THE SHORT SEASON* •
Produced, USIA/NATO, Naples Italy (1967),
New York Premiere, Cubiculo Theater (1970)
Selected scenes, Ch. 31, NY (1970)
• *THE APOCALYPSE ACCORDING TO J. J. (ROUSSEAU)* •
(Original Italian, by Mario Apollonio)
Original translation from the Italian by AP (1969)
Showcase production, The Classic Theater, NY (1975)
Selected scenes, Columbia University, NY (1975)
• *IN THE GREEN ROOM* •
Griffon House Publications, NY (2000)
• *CIPANGO!* (A short play in several sequences) •
(Available on videotape through Educational Video Co.)
• *MINIONS OF THE RACE** (Award-winning short play) •
• *INCIDENT AT THE GREAT WALL** •
• *THE ACTOR IN SEARCH OF HIS MASK** •
** IN *THREE SHORT PLAYS* (Introduction by Mario Fratti) •
Griffon House Publications, NY (1994)

AUTHOR'S PREFACE

The stories in this volume were written over a period of years but only recently brought together and edited for publication.

"Soho Revisited" takes place in an area of London familiar to both residents of the city and visitors. "A Tape for Bronko" is based on a month-long tour of Yugoslavia (where notices of roadway fatalities as described in the story were disconcertingly real). "Do Me a Favor" is in a category of its own, an unsolved "mystery." But whatever places and events nudged me into writing, the stories that emerged are my own creations, for which I must assume full responsibility.

Some of my characters, too, may seem familiar; but any resemblance to people living or dead is coincidental. They were created to fit the events described . . . although, almost always, they knew who they were before I did.

NEW YORK CITY
JANUARY, 2001

FOR HENRY

A TAPE FOR BRONKO

The name finally began to register on my second day in Belgrade. Perhaps it was the massive back, the thick neck rising from it, the solid squarish head above it that made me hear "Bronko." It was weeks later that I got it straight. But by then, my first impressions had taken root and the original name stuck.

Coming off the plane I was too busy greeting my hosts to notice him. Later there was the usual confusion of introductions, sorting out of luggage, getting people into cars for the drive back to the city. My eyes were heavy and my whole body ached from the long flight from New York and the two-hour stopover in Paris; but knowing my friend E.B. (who was my official Embassy host in Belgrade), I knew I would have to stay awake into the small hours of the morning. He and his wife had planned a cocktail party and dinner that night, to welcome me.

It was only when I had finally settled back in the embassy car, clutching the month-long itinerary that was thrust into my hands somewhere along the line, that I became aware of Bronko. My first view of the back of his head was through a tired mist. He eased effortlessly into the heavy traffic. Seen from behind, his broad shoulders and large head scarcely moving, his eyes focused straight ahead, his huge hands resting on the wheel with authority and confidence, they too scarcely moving, he reminded me of a robot.

From where I sat behind the passenger seat, I found myself watching him. He seemed unaware of my scrutiny. He drove with total concentration, a restrained intensity, as though life itself depended on him, turning his head slightly only when absolutely necessary to check the side view mirror. His hands on the wheel were those of a peasant: pudgy, fleshy, but not soft. Like the rest of him they were quite large and, at first, seemed formless – a grotesque enlargement of baby-fat fingers and thick round wrists. That first impression was misleading, I realized soon enough. He was all muscle; no doubt he could have killed a man with one blow. (Later I learned that he had, in fact, killed several Germans, as a partisan during the war.)

Everything about him was solid, tough. The black Chevelle he drove for the Embassy took on vibrations of greatness in response to the changing of gears; accelerating on a clear stretch of road, it rumbled its satisfaction. The Chevelle in action was an extension of Bronko's own self-assurance. They were made for each other.

I learned very quickly to appreciate the disciplined economy with which he used the five-gear stick shift, never relaxing, not even on the level stretches. Occasionally he smoked – first turning ever so slightly and raising his head to look into the rear view mirror for my nod – always with the same intense concentration, savoring every breath. And how he enjoyed weaving in and out of the caravans of slow-moving vans and old trucks, racing up blind curves on the wrong side of the road to pass a presumptuous *seicento* Fiat as it strained along, trying to uphold its dignity! The Chevelle responded well to his arrogance, energized by his display of authority. I tried to relax and enjoy it.

A few days after my arrival, Bronko drove me for meetings in Novi Sad. On the way, he pointed several times, with jabbing motions of his forefinger, to the cellophane-wrapped wreaths hanging on trees by the roadway to mark – he informed me each time – the spot where a "road fatality" had taken place. The only irony was in the smile I resisted. He was much too wholesome to indulge in hidden parallels.

He was to pick me up again in two days, when my business in Novi Sad was done. On the appointed morning, he arrived three hours early. I was writing some cards while waiting in the lobby of the Varadin Hotel for my luncheon host, Prof. N., when Bronko strolled in. My surprise, at seeing him there so early, must have registered. When I rose to greet him and dropped some of the cards, he stooped to pick them up, handed them back to me and said, in his heavily-accented English, all the while nodding his reassurance, "Don't worry, I wait." I suggested he could have lunch while he waited. He nodded again, with a small smile, holding up his hand as though to ward off any further comments, and started to move away. "Have your lunch, then," I persisted. "Don't worry," he repeated. "I eat." I wondered if he meant present, past, or future. A little while later, I caught sight of him propped up on one of the stools in the miniature bar of the hotel, just off the lobby, sipping a beer. Still later, as I went in to lunch with my host, I saw Bronko settling down at a small table near the entrance to the dining room. I smiled in relief as he tucked a napkin under his chin.

I finally got his name right one night at dinner, when M.B., my host's wife, corrected me. She leaned across the table and, in her southern drawl, her head cocked to one side, her long blonde hair threatening to fall over her eye said: "Sweetie, it's Svenko." She spelled it for me. "Why can't you get it right?" I decided it would take too long to explain. In any case, by that time the name Bronko and the image it called up were indissolubly one. I could no more relinquish the name than I could betray the impressions that had evoked it. Oh, I made sure that "Svenko" had registered, but it was only a concession to public formality. For me, it was still "Bronko."

The morning I left for an eight-day trip through southern Yugoslavia, Bronko was there to drive me to the airport. I was all packed and just about ready to leave when I remembered a small battery-operated tape recorder my host had offered to lend me for the trip. I took it, thinking it might be useful for quick notes, when things were still fresh in my mind; but when I tested it I discovered the batteries were dead. Bronko disappeared without a word and returned in a matter of minutes with new batteries. They proved to be the wrong kind. He left again and came back with a new batch. God only knows where he got them at seven in the morning! When the machine finally came to life, I smiled and nodded my head in appreciation. He nodded back, his eyes half-closed, pleased by my reaction, but with an expression that clearly said: "Did you really think I would let you down?"

I was so grateful for his gruff attention and so taken with his quiet competence that I placed the recording machine away with exaggerated care . . . and left my passport behind. It cost me an extra day in Pristina, while frantic calls were made to the embassy in Belgrade. In spite of the inconvenience, I felt strangely pleased: a small price to pay for Bronko's selfless optimism! Only later, as I settled back in the car for the long drive back to Belgrade, did I remember that I had completely forgotten to use the tape recorder. I was shattered. What would I say to Bronko if he asked about it? A dozen excuses flitted through my mind, but none of them seemed worthy. It did occur to me that Bronko probably wasn't expecting me to say anything. Still, I was bent on finding something to put on that tape recorder — not so much for Bronko's sake, I thought at the time, but for my own.

I was jolted back to the present by the slamming of brakes and realized that I might not have the chance to say or do anything at all, ever again! In place of Bronko, another driver, M., had been assigned to get me back to Belgrade, since he was coming north anyway, to pick up a government official who was returning to Skopje. Now, he came to a screeching stop as he attempted to pass a huge van loaded with crates of peppers. Oncoming cars flashed their lights in warning as he skidded back into the other lane, just in time to avoid a major collision. I sat very still, stiff with apprehension. In my mind's eye I saw those black wreaths that had accumulated in my memory, the battered wrecks that had been left on the grass near the road somewhere near Pristina, all the black-edged notices on the hundreds of trees we had passed, grim warnings to motorists. In my overheated imagination I pictured the notes, cards, and manuscripts in my briefcase, the tape recorder as well, strewn over the road to be gathered up eventually by the farmers and peasants, arranged into a display (with my full name, titles, and degrees in gold on a wide satin ribbon), the final work of art hung on a nearby tree. I pictured Bronko pointing out the spot to some other American visitor.

I muttered something under my breath. M. didn't know a word of English; but the guide/interpreter who had been sent along and sat beside him, heard my sarcastic remark and half-turned to answer, somewhat sharply, that his colleague "was not a frustrated racing champion but a *professional* driver!" I mumbled something by way of an apology, reminding myself that the man was just an ordinary human being, no doubt likeable enough in other circumstances, with a family who cherished him, and really no worse a driver than so many others on the road —

He was a short thin wiry man with a tremendous appetite. I can still see him eating with noisy gusto, his head bent low over his plate. He devoured the sports news in the same way, bent low over the page as though he had to eat the words in order to grasp their meaning. These moments of rest, innocuous enough, simply added fuel to my irrational antipathy. At such times, I would resist the temptation to blurt out my impatience by trying to picture him at home with his wife and children, sitting at the head of the dining table, lord of his domain. Surely he must have some redeeming qualities! At lunch in Sopocina, I watched him wipe his mouth after a full meal, laughing all the while with his friend, the guide. "He is saying," my interpreter informed me, "that he requires very little in life, only three things — good food, good wine, and . . . er, large-bosomed women." M., his own best audience, slowly repeated the phrase in his own language, relishing it all over again. I smiled weakly and said something about a wife's predictable response to his comment. They both laughed uproariously, nodding appreciatively at me, as though I had joined them in some sort of sordid private conspiracy. My last illusion had been cruelly shattered: M had no wife. He was just a boor, a lecher, a lousy driver.

I had very little time to brood. After a wrong turn near Sopocina (it cost us an extra hour on a dirt road, with peasants staring at us as we invaded their territory), he stopped abruptly to ask directions. In so doing, he swerved to the right and landed in a ditch. He tried to back up precipitously while I held my breath, expecting the muffler to be ground loose in his noisy effort to regain the road. His confidence was maddening. Neither he nor his friend the interpreter made any effort to get out and push, or to recruit for the purpose some of the younger men who had gathered around to watch.

My last tense moments came just outside Pristina, when M. passed a bus and remained on the other side of the road until an oncoming car flashed its lights and, in panic, came to an abrupt stop on the narrow shoulder. I can still see the shocked face of the other driver turning to stare at us zooming past. My guide muttered something, but M. simply shrugged and with a dramatic turn moved back into our lane.

Behind the wheel, he literally squirmed, hunched over it in the same way he hunched over his food and newspaper. He took the turns with his right arm raised high, elbow out, tracing a sweeping half circle. Invariably, he would smooth his hair with his left hand or scratch his left ear as he came out of a turn. When he passed other cars, he would announce his intention with a grunt, then press down on the horn. Alongside the other vehicle, he would turn to look at the occupants with a supercilious air, slowing down to relish his triumph. If we passed a woman on the road, especially a young peasant girl carrying a load of wood or balancing milk pails on her shoulders, he would turn slowly, following her with his eyes as far as he could.

Bumping along the narrow mountain strip between Solonica and Pristina, my frustration growing every minute and threatening to explode as M. raced along the thin macadam edge between the rising cliff on the left and the unprotected drop on the right, I suddenly knew how I would use the tape recorder. I would describe M. at the wheel — and give Bronko the tape as a gift when I got back. He wasn't likely to grasp my full intention, my veiled appreciation of his skill, or the therapeutic value the gesture had for me; he probably wouldn't even play the tape through; but if nothing else, he would be flattered at receiving it. My little gift would serve us both.

Sure in my purpose, my mind quickly targeted the several other drivers who might be included in my caustic appraisal. They shot up, one after the other, on the screen of my frustrated silence: . . . the tall dark French-Italian Slovene, with his pencil-thin moustache and two gold teeth, who drove me from Dubrovnik to Sarajevo in a sleek brown Mercedes, talking for most of seven hours in his broken Italian; . . . the university "assistant" who invited me to his room for tea; . . . the fellow who collected Elvis Presley records and handed me a list of titles he wanted me to search out and send him from the States; . . . the retired colonel who wanted me to file a patent for him but wouldn't tell me what it was for . . . .

Just outside Belgrade I must have dozed off . . . . "A little something for you," I heard myself say to M. and held out a black wreath. He shook his head: "No, no, we're only allowed to accept tapes," he said and reached into the back of the car to take mine. "That's Bronko's tape," I told him, snatching it away. Then suddenly Bronko was helping me out of the car. "It's all right," he said, nodding reassuringly. "The batteries are dead." He broke open the cassette and hung the wreath, decorated with long strands of discarded tape, on a near-by tree.

DO ME A FAVOR

I rested my hand on his hair, cut short, the color of dirty snow. I thought, the winter earth would look like this from a plane.

My hand slipped a little, then fell. It was like falling off the edge of the world. "I have to catch a plane," I said. Neither of us moved.

"I'll call a cab." He stood there examining his nails.

"It was good seeing you after, what? Six years?"

"Seven and a half. I came by your place with my mother, remember? Your sweet sixteen party. You lived in Larchmont. We had a hard time finding your house, and your mom scolded us for being late."

I laughed. I had forgotten. He looked up frowning.

"Will you do something for me?"

"Shoot."

"My wife Emma."

I stared. "Come again?"

"Shoot my wife Emma."

He didn't blink once. He just stood there and waited for an answer.

"You can't mean what I think I just heard," I said.

"You heard right." He became animated then. "I've got it all worked out. Trust me. It's like any other piece of business I take on. And I'm very good at what I do."

"Then why don't you take this on too?"

"The spouse is always the prime suspect."

"What about relatives, house guests, acquaintances, friends? Aren't they going to be suspects, too? Won't they be questioned?" I heard my words coming at me from a distance, as though someone else was speaking them.

"No one will think of questioning you. If they do, you'll be hundreds of miles away within a few hours."

"Oh? Where am I going?"

"Back to the States."

"I have two weeks to go yet."

"You can come back any time you like."

"Really?" I threw down my coat and tote on the nearest chair. I crossed my arms and studied his face for a few seconds. Then I took a deep breath and said:

"I work at a very demanding job. I saved up enough vacation time and money to spend a month in Italy and France. It was nice running into you. You have a great place here. The party you gave for me last night was a real surprise. I enjoyed it. We had a chance to catch up on things. I knew Aunt Millie had died last year, but your talking about her brought back some good memories when our families used to get together in the summers." I raised my hand to ward off any interruption. "But when I get back to the States, and that won't be until two weeks from now, because I'm not cutting this trip short for anyone, least of all for a distant relative – "

"Cousin. Our grandmothers were sisters – "

" – a distant relative who I happened to run into while I was having coffee outside my hotel and who wants me to shoot his wife, . . . when I get back, these three days will be erased from memory. Got that? What it means is that I never want to hear from you again." I was angry.

He seemed strangely calm. My words had not made much of an impact.

"Later, you can come as often as you like."

"Oh?" I meant it sarcastically, but it came out a real question. "I'm not quite on your level. I can't take time off whenever I feel like it, even if I could afford it!"

"You won't ever have to work again."

Again, I stared. He had a way about him. I couldn't quite figure out why I was still standing there, listening to him. I was beginning to feel something else, too. I was afraid. Not of him, but of my curiosity.

"Will you call me a cab, please?" He looked at me as though waiting for some signal. "Look," I said, impatiently, "I'm your guest. I'm stuck here in the middle of Nowhere, France. I want to leave and catch my flight to Lyon. I have friends waiting for me there."

I didn't really expect him to do it, but he surprised me by walking to the phone and speaking softly into it in French. He put down the receiver and turned to me.

"I meant it," he went on, ignoring the interruption. "You'll never have to work again."

"Just like that."

"I've opened a Swiss account in your name. It has a token sum of $100,000 in it as a starter. A parting gift."

I had to admire his style. I had no doubt what he said was true.

"You know what I'm saying is true," he went on, as though he had read my mind. "In a day or two, there will be ten million dollars in your account."

I tried to take it in. Was he insane? Mom had often said her cousin Millie was a bit strange.

"Your mother must have told you that I made lots of money over the last four years. When my father died, I inherited a mess of things. I wasn't really good at anything, but I decided to play around with what I had. It was a game at first. It became a curse. I didn't need it, want it, but money came in with every breath I took. It was something to do, something to keep me from thinking too long about other things. Rich or poor, my life is the same."

"You wouldn't have all this if you were poor," I waved my hand in a grand, philosophic gesture.

"I can live without it. It was Emma's idea. I need very little. I don't have the usual vices. I use my money to make my friends happy."

"But not your wife." He didn't answer. Instead, he took my hand and led me into the beautiful drawing room to the right of the marble staircase that faced the entrance. He drew me, like a parent gently pulling a child, to the large windows overlooking the south side of the estate. He pulled back the curtain with his free hand and opened the windows, first one then the other. He did this without letting go of my hand. The fragrance of roses wafted in. Outside, the bright summer lawn sloped down and beyond it was the breathtaking view of the ocean. I had stood in that very spot, admiring it all, the day I arrived. I was impressed all over again, standing there now.

"Beautiful, isn't it. Oh, I enjoy this place. But I can live without it." He paused briefly. "When I wake up in the morning and see her sprawled on the bed next to me, I want to die. The air around me is poisoned when she's there. Even just thinking of her makes my flesh crawl."

"Hey, nobody forced you to marry her."

"She did. She told me she was pregnant."

"Nobody gets married these days just because they goofed."

"Here it's different. Besides, I thought it was time to think about a family."

"So it *was* your choice," I said with a grim smile. "Do you plan to make it a habit? You'll need all your money for that."

"Don't be flippant, Kootie." It was the first time in the three days I'd been in his house that he had addressed me with my old nickname. I had almost forgotten it myself. It was my childish mispronunciation of "cutie." I was about four. Someone was visiting dad, and as the visitor was leaving Mom came downstairs with me. The man leaned down and stroked my hair. "So you're Katie," he said. And I had corrected him, "No. My name is Kootie Pie."

"When I married her she was like Botticelli's Venus. Everyone would turn to stare. Now . . . well, you met her. She never gets up before one or two in the afternoon. Then she disappears until dinner, if there are guests. Otherwise she just disappears."

"So she's gained some weight, drinks more than she should. She likes to insult you in public. It's still no reason to kill her. Just get a divorce, for godssake!"

"Our family goes back quite a way, you know that. And there's never been a divorce."

"There's never been a murder, either."

"Ah, you're wrong there, but no, not recently."

"I can't believe you're serious."

Outside, a car had pulled up in the driveway. He came away from the window and sat down on one of the soft-cushioned sofas. I went on, still by the window, my mind and heart racing:

"You want to kill your wife and here I am, a widow at twenty-four, who'd do anything to get Frank back!"

"You can have him back any time."

My mouth must have dropped open. I turned from the window and leaned against the wall. My lips felt dry. Outside, the driver honked several short bursts.

"So, you're Christ now. You raise the dead."

"No, the living." Oh, he was full of surprises.

I closed my eyes, my heart pounding. I rested my head against the wall and took deep breaths. When I opened my eyes, he was beside me with a tall glass of water. I turned away from those searching, untroubled eyes.

"Here, drink this." He stood by as I gulped down the water. "Why don't you sit down?" When I didn't move, he went on. "He's alive. There's a new woman."

I couldn't get any words out. I simply shook my head in disbelief. Outside, we could hear the taxi drive off after one last impatient blast of the horn.

"I wasn't going to say anything. What's the point? It's almost two years. I thought you'd gotten over it. But since you brought it up — "

Without opening my eyes I said: "But the plane crashed. The plane he had been flying."

"Yes, just after take-off in Marseilles."

My eyes suddenly flew open. "How do you know all this? What else did you find out?"

"Oh, I do my homework. I don't get into anything without doing some research. Even this, yes . . . . " For a moment he seemed ill at ease, but it was only a fleeting impression. "Since we're at it . . . . I didn't run into you the other day. I knew you were coming, found out where you were staying. The other morning I waited for you to come down for breakfast. I came up to you as you were drinking your coffee."

I heard the words but they registered dimly. My mind was elsewhere.

"So you researched Frank?"

"Actually, no. I found out by accident." The look on my face must have reflected disbelief because he went on quickly, "I was scanning quarterly reports of companies I do business with, glancing at new names added to their board of directors, things like that. Last year, one company had replaced two directors. I didn't have a clue at the time, but I did what I always do. I asked one of my assistants to compile a brief background resume of the new people. I like to know who I'm dealing with. It was purely routine." He paused before going on.

"One of them was from Berlin, the other living outside of Paris but originally from the States. I followed both leads and discovered, oh never mind the details. What you want to know is, he's changed his name and started a business that's doing pretty well. He's made new contacts. They have a child, a boy. He's almost a year old."

After a while, I said: "They're living together, isn't that what you said?"

"No, I said . . . ."

This time I didn't let him finish. "They're married?"

"Yes."

I went back to sit on the couch and he followed. We sat in silence across from one another for what seemed an eternity. Thoughts banged against the cavity that was my head. Feelings I didn't recognize and didn't like exploded deep inside me, bursts of flames, white heat enveloped my insides, my stomach churned as in a storm, my nerve ends prickled right down to my toes, as when Dr. Forman drew blood from me for the very first time, when I was fourteen.

Suddenly I was angry. "But he died in the plane crash. Just outside the airport!" At first, I didn't think he was going to answer, but then he said softly, looking down at the floor, his hands clasped between his legs:

"No, someone else died. Soon after the crash, the dispatcher retired. You figure it out. The log, the report, carried your husband's name. He had hired the plane. No one came forward to deny it or question it. The body was so badly burned even the teeth were no big help. Besides, there was no need to go any further with it. His name was registered as having taken the plane out. He never came home. He was for all we knew, quite dead."

"But the other man . . ."

"No one reported anyone missing. And, whatever else you're thinking, forget it. We'll never know why someone else took the plane up. In any case, it was ruled an accident. I think your husband simply took advantage of an incredible piece of good luck." I must have groaned, because he reached across and put his hand on mine.

"From his point of view, it may have seemed so." He pulled back and crossed his legs. "You *can* get him back if you really want him. He's still legally married to you."

I must have tried to laugh. It came out a gurgling sound. I managed to get some words out. "What I'd like to get back is the last two years of my life." I frowned. "How do I know what you're telling me is true?" I knew what he would say before he said it.

"Because you know I don't lie. You know I have never lied to you. I haven't lied once since we started this conversation. Why should I?"

He was right, of course.

"Two years! Two whole years thinking he was dead, mourning him!"

"Did you really? Mourn him?"

I shot up from the sofa and paced to the window and back. "You're a terrible man," I told him when I had regained control. "Nothing touches you!" I stood over him, struggling to keep my composure.

"That's not true," he said. "I know you're hurt. But not for the reason you think."

"Whatever our differences," I went on, trying to stay calm, "they were unimportant. What was important to me was the promise we made, the pledge we had taken. We cared for one another. We swore to build a life together."

"But your heart wasn't really in it." He held up a warning hand. I held back what I was about to say. "You made that very clear," he went on softly, almost gently. "Just now you said 'differences,' 'promise,' 'pledge,' 'cared for one another,' 'swore to build a life together.' Not once have you mentioned love, happiness. Did you love him? Did he love you? Were you happy together?"

I shook my head, like a dog shaking off water. "Love! Love obviously comes and goes. He made that clear enough!"

"No no. *You* made it clear. *You* wanted something else. I'm not criticizing you. But it's true, isn't it? You wanted security, a family, a routine. Love was a foolish thing to build on. And you may be right." I said nothing. He went on. "You can understand why I felt it was best to leave things alone under the circumstances. He seems serene where he is, with the new family he has created for himself. And you still have a very good chance to get what you want, whatever it is you feel you need." He came across to sit beside me and lifted my head. "Look at me and tell me I'm wrong." I couldn't speak.

After a while, he sat back and just looked at me. When he talked again, it was almost a whisper. "Strange how lives cross, people come together, separate, come together again. The patterns are predictable, you know. There are only a few and they cover just about all possible human behavior." He gave a bitter laugh. "Oh, yes, I've researched that too. I'm afraid I don't hold much hope for the human race. I have a theory you see, aside from all that has been said," he gestured with his hand, a large sweep that took in the entire room, the world, the universe. "I don't believe man is top of the heap, that God singled him out for special privileges on this planet or any other planet. We think of ourselves as unique, in a special category as humans, but what sort of God would give us all the goodies we enjoy — art, lust, music, new technology, exotic foods, all those things that we like to think make life worth living — what God would give all that and then destroy us? We're human, after all, we are told. What we mean is, we die like the other animals. We can't get around that!

"But if that's so," he went on, searching my face, his eyes glittering with a powerful emotion I couldn't quite take in, "if all that is true, why don't we act like other animals? Instead, our pleasures fade and we have to pump them up with perverse priming. Animals mate when nature tells them. They eat only when they're hungry; they don't stuff themselves or go looking for excitement out of season, for anything that appeals to them, any time, day or night. By contrast with animals, our so-called sensibilities are nothing more than highly developed nerve-ends that respond to our acquired perversities. There's nothing natural about the human race, unless you call our gorging on pleasures, natural. We take what we want and justify the havoc we wreak on the grounds that, as the highest form of intelligence, we enjoy special privileges. We've even created an invisible overseer to authorize all this. I call it self-indulgence writ large." He frowned at some idea that had intruded, then went on.

"It's an old story. I've added nothing. We're just a fluke. We've even learned how to justify our self-serving behavior by creating morality. It all started with the great Socrates." He burst out laughing, a harsh sound, then went on almost breathlessly: "Just so we can lord it over all other things around, grab what we want in the name of some divine purpose." He leaned across, bringing his face close to mine. "We're a big joke!"

I was riveted to the look on his face. It glowed with a kind of religious fanaticism, and, yes, a suggestion of madness too. At the same time, I must have taken in every word he said because I remembered that conversation long after. I wanted desperately to get away but couldn't move.

"The taxi came and went," I said weakly.

He looked at me with the same wild intensity with which he had delivered his brief lecture and then burst out laughing, a rather pleasant laugh this time. "So, I didn't impress you?" He picked up my coat and tote. "I'll drive you to the airport myself. You won't miss your plane."

I followed him out into the bright sunlight, on to the gravel driveway. I looked out over the wide expanse of garden, with its graceful gazebo on one side, the beautiful fountain with its *carrara* cupids on the other. The burst of colors was like a rich Renaissance painting. I glanced behind me at the chateau for one last look as he brought the Mercedes around.

We drove in silence, but there was tension between us. It was probably my fault. At the same time I was acutely aware of some inner struggle he was experiencing. My own nerves were raw. I felt drained. At the airport, he called a porter and watched as my luggage was checked in. He took both my hands in his. A rueful smile played around his lips.

"I won't try to apologize or excuse myself. I meant every word I said." He dropped my hands and kissed me quickly on the cheek. "Don't judge me, please. I haven't judged *you*."

"I have nothing to be ashamed of," I countered lamely.

"Nonsense. We all have secrets, we're all weak."

Just as I turned to leave, he said: "What are you going to do about your husband?" I had no answer, but he must have read something in my face because the look he gave me was sharp, a kind of warning. "Don't rush into anything," he said crisply. "He's not worth it. And in any case, you're not exactly free of blame." I wanted to slap him. Instead I stood there struggling for words.

"You said you didn't judge me."

"I don't. I never will. What I'm telling you, you already know, deep down inside. Look at the plus. You've gotten rid of him. Much easier than my case. I still have to work mine out. I should be as lucky as you!"

I knew I was doing something I would regret. He was telling the truth and I didn't want to hear it. But I slapped him anyway. He grinned. It was the only time I'd seen him do that. He suddenly seemed much younger than his thirty-two years. I didn't trust myself to say anything more, so I turned and walked away. I felt his eyes on me but I didn't want to give him the satisfaction of looking back. I walked straight into the terminal. After I'd checked in, I sat at the bar and had a martini. When the flight was called, my mind was almost blank. I didn't want to recall any part of my visit to the chateau. My cousin receded into the dim past. My husband was dead and buried.

I had to believe that he had been killed.

I had to believe the body I'd buried was his, what was left of it.

I had to believe I had not made a horrible mistake.

I had to believe —

The little voice I was trying to stifle finally spoke up. It had a curious resemblance to my cousin's voice.

Why are you closing up like this? It's no good. You'll have to live with it, you know.

Or, I could report him to the proper authorities. I could denounce him as a bigamist. He would lose his job, maybe the woman too, if she didn't know about his past, about me. About our marriage. He'd go to jail. Then what? What satisfaction would I find in doing that? What about his child?

What about his child? the voice asked. *Have you thought of him, the little boy? Are you going to feel any better doing all those things?*

No. Yes. I wasn't sure. Then, the dam burst and I was sobbing. The flight attendant was coming through the cabin. He leaned over the other passenger, an elderly man reading *The Wall Street Journal*.

"Anything I can do?" asked the flight attendant.

"Nothing, nothing," I said quickly with a forced smile. I waved him away and took out some Kleenex to blow my nose, wipe the tears from my cheeks and neck. I tried to keep my thoughts at bay, but it didn't work. Against that emptiness, what had happened and what lay ahead suddenly flashed before me, crowding out the present: my friends waiting for me in Lyon, my job back home, the high-rise in mid-town Manhattan, where my husband and I had lived for almost a year; my cousin asking me to kill his wife, the bank account with ten million dollars. It had happened. He had said all those things. They were all true.

Much later, just before flying back to the States I pulled out the small paper I'd found in my tote, where he had put it before we parted. I called the bank listed there and asked for information about the account in my name. They didn't give me any. I was relieved, convinced that it had been closed.

But three months after my return to New York, I received a letter from my cousin. There was no return address just the postmark of the town where he lived on the Riviera. In it, he gave me instructions about how to access my Swiss account. There was a postscript. "I said it was a gift. No strings attached. Enjoy it. You deserve something special." I put it aside and soon forgot it.

Then, at the beginning of the new year, I was promoted to the executive level job I had been waiting for. My first assignment as Assistant Head of Public Relations took me to Paris, where I met with a group of Japanese clients. The firm had chosen me because I spoke Japanese as well as French. I knew the protocol too. I'd taken a short seminar not long before, on cultural networking. In fact, I had been seeing quite a lot of James Thressich, the man who headed the communications group our firm had hired to train its executives in protocol procedures.

I was returning to my hotel on the last evening of my stay in Paris, mission accomplished, quite satisfied with myself and with some new personal contacts I had made, when something caught my eye. I picked up the evening paper at the corner kiosk and read in French about the inquest that had taken place the day before to determine the cause of a mishap in which the wife of noted billionaire industrialist _____ _____ was killed while negotiating a curve on the Amalfi road, near Naples. Most of the story was a rehash of what apparently had been printed some days earlier. Emma had been visiting friends and was driving back, alone, to her hotel in Naples. It was growing dark. She missed a turn, the car swerved then fell into the side of the cliff, turning a number of times before hitting bottom. The story had lots of fillers about my cousin's business, his wealth, how he came into his money, how everything he touched seemed to prosper. I read the account over and over again, not at all surprised to learn that the inquest had ruled Emma's death "an accident." The story ended: "Not everything can be bought."

I remember laughing hysterically for a minute or two. Then, in spite of my effort to distance myself from the event and from everything else I knew, the past came surging back like a rogue wave, drowning my resolve.

He'd done it! Or was it really an accident? Even if I wanted to do so, what exactly could I report? I had the weird feeling I was caught in the same trap as before.

Slowly, that too slipped from my mind. Much later, almost two years to the day I read that newspaper story, I received a short note from my cousin. He'd moved, sold the chateau, lived now in Paris, where he had his main headquarters, was thinking of visiting the States and would I still be at the same address? He'd like to see me again.

For days, then weeks, I debated whether to answer or not. Finally, I tore up the note. There was no point seeing him. What would we talk about? How he got away with it? Or did he want to reassure me it was really an accident? I felt he had left his mark on me. I could never shake him off. But I didn't have to see him again, ever. Whatever the message he intended to bring, I did not want to have to hear it. I hated myself for not being able to act rationally in the matter, but there it was. The truth was, I was afraid of seeing him, of reading whatever was there, in his face.

I had moved in with James, some months earlier, but the mail addressed to my old place was still being forwarded to me. That's how I learned that my husband had been killed. The envelope had a Paris postmark but no return address. This time there was no note even, just a clipping from a French newspaper. It reported a shooting in a suburb of Paris. There was an argument in the street. Two people had been killed. One was the man who had started the quarrel, the other an innocent bystander who had tried to stop it. He had received one of the fatal bullets intended for the other man. There was a photo taken of Frank in some place in the country, probably where he lived with his wife and child. He was smiling, his head half turned away, as though caught by surprise. He seemed happy.

I looked at the picture for a long time, with sadness mostly and a feeling of emptiness for things past, precious years lost. I thought of Frank, who had been my husband, who had found a way to get rid of me, who had found happiness. I was free too, now, I could be happy. Was my cousin happy? Had he married again? They say one chooses always the same type of partner. If so, had he found a new Emma, just as beautiful, just as disappointing? How many Botticelli Venuses would he go through before settling into his own shortcomings?

Finally I had to face up to what was really nagging at me.

Was Frank's death really just a coincidence? I didn't think so, but I couldn't bring myself to entertain the other possibilities. At that moment, I was almost tempted to invite my cousin to visit me, after all. I felt there were a lot more questions I wanted — no, needed — to ask him. I dispelled the thought even as it surfaced, telling myself that the only reason I was toying with the idea of his coming to see me was that I had thrown away his address and knew I couldn't reach him easily any more.

Oh, but you do want to see him, said the little voice inside me, not so innocent any more. *He's worked it all out.*

Had he found love?

Had he found happiness?

Had he stumbled on something worth all that old trouble?

You're afraid he won't share it with you this time.

What is happiness?

What is love?

I knew with certainty, then, that I would never want to hear the answers.

PLAY IT AGAIN!

Who was it said we're free only when we know we're puppets?

Well, whoever it was, was *right!* Why else would I be lying here so calmly, soaked in my own sweat, pumped dry again? Sure I'm free. I'm free to come and go. Tomorrow our friendly shrink, Dr. Bergstrom, will sit down, cross his legs, and tell me I never learn, girl, never learn! But I have. I've learned a lot, Doc . . . . I've learned that you're as much a puppet as I am. You're addicted to getting people to depend on you forever, isn't that right? Making them over into what you think is their best image. Like Daddy. Each time he tries to force me into his fantasy of what I should be like, poof! I disappear. He's still trying and I'm still running. I'll bet he's already been here to claim me again, right? Well, it won't work this time either. Or is this my new home sweet home? Will little Miss O.D. make it with the help of Big Bird Daddy and Bruce Willis in Doc's white coat? Time creaks past and leaves me stranded. Just the way I want it. So, play it again, only this time cut out the crap. Let's not fool around anymore.

God, I miss Daisy. Wonder if she's still in Newark, in the house where her big sister Laureen used to live. Big, all right! Always *big.* It's my livelihood, she'd say laughing and patting her swollen belly. It was fun visiting Laureen. She always had a fix for us if we were really desperate. All the luck, to have family like that.

Once, when we there alone, on a high (Laureen had gone to the Welfare office to complain about something), we ate the fish in the tank. Laureen had a fit. She loved those exotic fish more than her babies, I think. Sometimes she'd lie down, dangling her legs over the side of the sofa, and watch them swimming in the tank — when she wasn't entertaining her boyfriends. Her babies were her income, but the fish were some kind of fantasy.

You're O.K. for a white creep, she'd say to me, smiling with those big teeth of hers, but don't push your luck. Once she really got mad when Daisy, yelling about something, kicked one of the neighbor's cats. Laureen was crazy about animals. I swear, she'd rather play with those cats and stare at her fish than take care of her kids. Her really big ambition in life, though, was to get a pet monkey and carry it around on her back. (No pun intended!)

So one day I told her the story of the monkey and the two old maids. (I read it years ago for a course I had to take in Italian at Queens College. I forget the author, but I figured he was easier than reading Dante.) At first I wasn't sure I should tell her the story, because, well, it's all right if you're Catholic, there are things you don't mind, like family jokes inside the family, but Laureen was a Baptist. I mean, outsiders might judge it badly. But one evening, when she was alone with us (no visitors had shown up), she was so depressed — this was right about the time we had eaten those exotic fish and she had not replaced them yet — that I decided to tell her the story. After that, she wanted to hear it every time she saw me. Laughed until she peed. "Tell my friend," she'd say, if some guy was there. There must be hundreds of men walking around with pieces of that story crowding their brains. Laureen heard it so many times, she could almost recite it herself after a while. But the first time, she kept interrupting. Nothing but questions, questions, questions.

Two old maids lived alone in a small town in Italy with their pet, a monkey they had raised from birth —

Laureen: "How did they get hold of a monkey?"

"What's the difference!"

They loved that monkey as though it was a member of the family. Early one morning, the older of the two sisters –

"You didn't say they were sisters."

"Well, they were."

– Clara was her name, discovered Zizzie, that was the monkey's name, sneaking out the back door. It went over the low brick wall that separated the sisters' house from the neighboring one and disappeared among the eucalyptus trees.

"You calypso? What hell kind of a tree is that?"

"Maples are maples? Well, these were eucalyptus. They have long leaves."

I picked up again:

The monkey was back in about forty minutes. The next morning, she and Fannie – she was the younger sister – stood by the window and watched Zizzie leave the house and disappear again among the eucalyptus. Same thing. Back in forty minutes or so. The third time it happened, the sisters decided to follow Zizzie and see where he went. They were careful to keep a certain distance, so Zizzie wouldn't see them and get upset. Then, as they came around the wall they saw the monkey disappear into the nearby church. It was still very early, around five o'clock. The church was empty, the first Mass wasn't scheduled until six-thirty.

"What's Mass?"

"It's like a revival meeting. Everybody prays, and sings, all that stuff. But the priest at Mass does magic tricks, too." Laureen knew about priests.

It was real early, the sun hadn't come up yet. The two sisters stepped inside and looked around the dark church. No sign of Zizzie. They crossed the vestibule and were –

"The what?"

"Vestibule! Foyer! The place at the back, just inside the door, before you walk down the aisle to the altar – "

"Ha ha! That'll be the day!?"

– they were just going to start down the aisle to look for Zizzie, when they saw him come out of one of the confessionals.

"What? What's that?"

"A booth, with just enough room for you to kneel. The priest sits right next to you, but there's a wall in between, and a screen, so he can't see who you are when you tell him your sins. Like going to a shrink, only it's free and the priest puts in a good word for you with God."

"Geez, Laureen, let her go on!" said Daisy.

"Who's stopping her?" said Laureen, waving me on.

Then, as the two sisters watched, their hands over their mouths as though keeping back the sound of their breathing, Zizzie went right up to the altar and started doing all the things that Father Gagnano does when he says Mass. The sisters stared as Zizzie went through all the motions. At one point they found themselves kneeling with the monkey, rising, crossing themselves, the whole bit. Until the monkey took out the chalice –

"Chalice?"

"A big gold cup –"

"Real gold?"

"Real gold."

"And what's inside?"

"Communion wafers. The priest holds them up, says some magic words, and then passes them around."

"What do they taste like?"

"They're just flour and water."

"That's it? Not even some cheese and pickles?"

"It's not real food. The priest has to forgive you your sins and bless you before you can have one. It's something special."

"All that trouble for a wafer that's not even real food? You call that special?"

"Geez, Laureen, at this rate, we'll be old maids ourselves by the time we get to the end!" said Daisy.

"Ha, ha! You, maybe, not me, sugar!"

I said: "Can I go on? The best part is yet to come!"

"So, go on!" said Laureen.

At that point, the sisters suddenly came to their senses.

"Why, what happened?"

"I just told you, Zizzie took out the chalice and — "

"Oh, O.K."

— he took out the chalice, bent over it as though praying, then raised it up high for a few seconds, put it down, knelt, made the sign of the cross over it, then, from a small table on the side of the altar, he picked up another chalice that usually held the wine —

"Ah, there's wine at least!"

"Only, there wasn't any wine yet. The altar boys who help out the priest at Mass bring that in later. The priest blesses it and it turns into the blood of Jesus."

"Wow? That's a good trick!" She was impressed.

Daisy waved me on:

Then the monkey ate the biggest of the wafers, a really big one, and drank down the wine.

"You said there wasn't any wine yet."

"He made believe he was drinking."

He did everything Father Gagnano did when he said Mass. Afterwards, Zizzie cleaned out the chalices, put them back where they belonged, and started up the aisle toward the entrance. The sisters quickly hid in one of the confession boxes so Zizzie wouldn't see them as he loped past. Later at home they debated what to do, whether they should tell Father Gagnano about it. They did, that same evening. The priest went crazy, told them the monkey had committed blasphemy and had to be destroyed.

"He's only a monkey," said Fannie, the younger one.

"He's just having some fun," said Clara.

"He's desecrated the altar," said Father Gagnano.

"But excuse me, Father," said Clara, "how can a monkey commit blasphemy? He's not baptized . . . ."

"He's not confirmed," said Fannie."

"He's a disgrace," said Father. "I don't know why the health officials let you keep him."

"But he's trained. The altar wasn't soiled — " said Clara.

"Not soiled, DESECRATED!" Father Gagnano repeated, his irritation showing by now. "I won't stand for that!"

"Really! All he was doing was imitating you! You should be flattered!" said Fannie, growing bold.

"Besides," said Clara, "if we all come from monkeys — "

"What!" shouted Father Gagnano, overturning his chair, as he jumped up. "WHAT!" His face was contorted, red as a beet.

After that, there was so much yelling that neither Fannie nor Clara remembered clearly what was said and who said it. The priest had stormed out of the rectory, and the two sisters knew they had to make a big decision. They certainly didn't like the idea of destroying their pet, so they packed a few things and rented a place in the periferia —

"Perry what?"

"The suburbs, like Long Island, Yonkers . . . . "

— where they could think things out quietly. It didn't take them long to reach a decision. They sold their house in town and with the money bought a small farm at the other end of the county. There they planted vegetables and bought some chickens. The main house was large and airy. The chicken coops were clean and neat. They even bought a cow and a dog to keep Zizzie company. Inside the big house, they set up a table where Zizzie could say his Mass every morning. Both Fannie and Clara made a point of attending, and after a while they even took from him the thin cracker that served as communion. (What harm could it do?) When Zizzie raised the round cracker to bless it, Clara swore she could almost distinguish the words — "This is my body."

"It can't hurt," said Fannie. "It's not as though we were not going to our own Mass in a real church . . . . "

In the summertime they would set up the altar outside, where the fruit trees heavy with peaches and cherries created a cool cathedral effect that was much appreciated by both sisters and insured them total privacy. Even had their neighbors, four miles away, decided to take a hike some morning at six, even if they were to find their way to where the high wall of the fruit trees began, even if they could have managed to get that close, they could never have reached the enclosure without making their presence known, because Napoleon, the large shaggy dog, barked at anything and everything that moved. He followed the two women everywhere and was always there beside them for Zizzie's Mass. Sometimes the new cow would crowd up close to the fence, but the gate was kept firmly shut, always, and she couldn't get out of the compound . . . .

You could tell Laureen loved that story. Because of the monkey, of course, but also because she liked to hear how the two old maids got around the priest (she had developed a violent dislike for Father Shaughnessy, from the local parish, after seeing him one afternoon, in his long black habit, playing soccer with the seventh-graders). Anyway, she liked the story and never got tired of listening to it. She loved animals, like I said, and getting a monkey of her own was her pet dream.

Watching her sometimes, her mouth open, her jaws working soundlessly as she listened to the details of Zizzie's blasphemy, I wondered if she had her own private fantasy about trailing clouds of glory from some kind of heavenly monkeyland. Or trailing *back* to it, like those ads where the water flows back into the faucet and Niagara Falls rises up to the top again, that kind of thing. Maybe we're all rolling back in time, to some new Platonic year. (I read that somewhere.) Wouldn't that be nice? To start all over again?

So, tell me, what's logical? An argument can point that way or this way. You know what? I think God would have gotten a kick out of Zizzie. We'll never know. We can't hear him laughing.

Besides, I think everything was figured out a long time ago. We just keep going through the motions, trying to keep from falling off the treadmill. In the end, we're all puppets struggling for definition. Teddy bears suffer their eyes to be torn out by grubby little fingers and live out their ignominy in silence. But monkeys, like children, bask in fantasies of puppet power. They don't know that it took a million or more years of exhaustion to fix this race to oblivion.

If only I could get it all down on paper, if I could use the typewriter. I don't have one, haven't had it for months; but even if I still had one, it wouldn't do me any good. Not now. Not ever. I'm buried alive in the hum of my ears. The desk lamp strikes me blind. My thoughts are forever stored in labeled cartons with the rest of the junk I left in Laureen's place and never bothered to pick up again. Letters ooze out of the crevices of my consciousness waiting for Wheel of Fortune.

Laureen would take care of me if she could, if she weren't dead. Two in the chest and one in the head. A lover's quarrel, the police report said. (Which of the guys, I wonder?) Whoever it was, he shot himself dead, too. That made me feel better. He must have really loved her. God, I miss her! If she were here now, she'd turn on the light in my head. Is Daisy living in that house? And the kids, who's loving them now?

I've zigzagged to something, but I can't make out what it is.

Oh, sure, I recognized daddy. When he came into the room, I made believe I was asleep. What can I say to him? When I was kid, well, sometimes he made me laugh. But he was never comfortable around me. I never quite figured out why. Who cares, anyway? Kids do better with people like Laureen, who love without reason and are loved back simply for being there, for laughing or crying, for trying to get away with whatever they can. Laureen loved her kids to death. When she tired of them, they hung around until she was ready for them again. They sensed her moods, gave her the space she needed. When she hit them, they cried out of love. She was their god, their world.

And she loved them back, even as she yelled at them. Kids feel those things. They don't love because they have to. They love even in the midst of violence, even as they watch strangers stagger out of mom's bedroom late in the morning, after a noisy night.

I loved Laureen that way. I felt like those kids of hers. Even in that cramped world, there was room for us, and we loved her in all her moods, drunk or sober, happy or angry. She flashed her sexuality like a beacon over a stormy sea. No one blamed her for being what she was. No one wanted to be towed to safety either. We basked in her all-consuming laser-sharp lust for life. We watched her take on whatever the day brought her.

And while I wait, stretched out on a stinking bed for that all-consuming flash when all sins turn to ashes, for the ceiling to be put back up there where it belongs, for the morning to etch me on a fresh white sheet like those outlines in the comics that go right through walls; while I wait for Mr. Clean to bathe me, spruce me up, tuck me into a squeaky new day, for Dr. Bergstrom (or whoever) to bring new medications, new promises, a new future; while I wait to find out if I still breathe or if I'm dead; while I lie here waiting, all I can think of is the perfect corpse, the ideal hospital, the conquest of paradise, Laureen's fish blupping their dreams in a bowl of carefully controlled and always freshened faith, a cat waiting to be stroked, Zizzie savoring the edge of a mystery.

Ah, but all filter systems break down at some point; sooner or later cats run off, monkeys grow old and die, with or without the sacraments, and old maids have nightmares about walls caving in, ceilings falling, floors fusing together in one huge giant crushing transparency.

Laureen would have kept the ceiling up there where it belongs. She dressed Zizzie in holiness. She could rewind the old film and make us feel it was the first time.

Why do I keep thinking of Laureen and the two old maids? Something pulls at the hem of my memory. In this narrow corridor of existence they come together, one heart and soul, their foibles irrelevant against the wide canvas of their common ground. I think of them as cosmic sisters, the fish and Zizzie and the cats and the babies as proof of their unexpressed conviction that there are no excuses to be made, no trying on sin for size. Whatever they did was largesse. Every moment was true and forever. They turned their daily renewal of self into irresistible magic, just as effective as Father Gagnano's Mass, when he turned bread and wine into something special.

I think the women had more in common than the priests as priests, you know what I mean? They had less pretensions about who they were, about what was right, who should be cast out, who or what might be salvaged within the small circle of providence. They knew who they were and accepted their frail humanity. If they were ever disappointed in what life dished out to them, they didn't knock anybody down out of spite or envy.

Don't try to pin me down again with what you call logic. Parents understand only their self-made self-imposed self-protective system of obligations. Why should children honor what they don't recognize as theirs? I couldn't give a shit who made me, where I came from. I might have been conceived in Tibet, in Alaska, back in the middle ages, back in dinosaur country. What difference would it make!

Laureen never wasted time searching her soul. She was her own miraculous creation. We could touch her, smell her, laugh with her, worry about her, back away from her wild stupor when she was under the influence, give her space when she was not all there, wait for her to unravel each twisted day of her life into some precious moments. I think I know what God would say. I know what daddy would say, too, but it's predictable and boring. The real question is, how did these words get trapped in this body? I could have been born a cockroach, or an Arctic wolf. What is this thing that looks out at the world through these eyes?

Who am I? There's a name on the I.D. around my wrist. Daddy thinks he knows. He filled out all the forms.

I am a golden bird cast in rigor mortis and wishing for anything but eternity or art!

Maybe tomorrow I'll go through the motions, give you what you want to hear. Maybe I'll even tell you a story.

Right now I have a question: How many monkeys say Mass on the point of a pin?

HALF A STORY,

A THIRD OF THE PIE

The big guy opened the door and stood to one side as Harry Delaney walked into the room. The man sitting behind the massive mahogany desk said something into one of the two phones on his desk and put down the receiver. He sat back in the large high-back leather chair and scrutinized the visitor. His smile did not reach his eyes. They were very dark brown, almost black, and the bushy eyebrows above them reinforced the effect the man had on even the most casual observer: *don't mess around with me.*

But Harry Delaney was not a casual observer. He had good reason to be worried.

"C'min, c'min Harry. . . . Sit down . . . . You know Bonz, Harry, he's been with me since his mother passed away." The large man stood to one side of the door, feet slightly apart, his hands folded in front of him. Dressed in a dark maroon tweed jacket, maroon shirt and black tie, he looked like a bouncer gone to seed. His hands were large and puffy. His face, heavily-pock-marked, had a grayish pasty tone, as though he rarely went out into the sun. His jacket was buttoned and bulged over his broad chest.

"When was that Bonz?" asked the man behind the desk, without taking his eyes from Harry. Bonz answered, his lips barely moving.

"Twelve years ago come Christmas eve."

At a wave from his host, Harry reluctantly sat down on the only other chair in the room, directly across from the desk.

"Yeah, God rest her soul," said the other. "Yeah, well, Bonz has been my right hand and my left hand all these years, right Bonz?" Bonz said nothing. The man at the desk lit a cigarette and took a deep breath. As an afterthought, he held it up and raised his eyebrows in a question. "Sorry. Would you like one?" Harry shook his head. "Yeah, I know," the other went on, as though they were two old chums waiting for take-out orders. "All my friends out there are quitting, and here I am, still puffing away. I guess until it happens you don't believe it ever will." He laughed at some hidden suggestion. "Anyway, I still got a few good years to think about giving it up." After taking another deep breath and exhaling the smoke slowly, with obvious relish, he rested the cigarette in a large crystal ashtray and leaned forward, crossing his arms on the desk in front of him.

"Well, Harry, I'm glad you're here. I was beginning to wonder. You were supposed to come yesterday — " Harry cleared his throat and moved slightly forward on the hard molded plastic seat. He was beginning to perspire. Now he spoke for the first time, uncertain, uncomfortable, knowing what was coming and knowing also he couldn't avoid it. He scarcely recognized his own voice.

"Like I said, on the phone, Joe, I'm really strapped. I need a few more days, three at most . . . . "

Joe watched him through narrowed eyes. When he spoke, his voice had a different timbre, the words came out sharp-edged. He sat back in his chair.

"Well, I tell you Harry, I've got a bit of a problem myself. Maybe we can help one another." He picked up the cigarette and puffed on it for a few seconds, all the while scrutinizing Harry across from him. When Harry didn't answer, Joe got up and walked across the room then back to where Harry sat. He looked down at him before going back to his desk, where he stood behind the leather chair, leaning into it slightly. The two men studied one another for a few seconds, then Joe waved his hand with a smile.

"Yeah, I could give you a bit more time to pay me back." Harry could not help betraying his relief, as Joe walked away from the desk again and went to stand near Bonz. Harry turned his head to follow his movements, not altogether sure what was coming. "But, to be honest with you, Harry, I don't think it'll do any good. As of today, you owe me the original five, plus two thousand interest, as we agreed, plus a penalty, as of today, of another thousand for being twenty-four hours late with your payment. You owe me, this minute, eight thousand dollars. By next week, that will have more than doubled. Will you have that kind of money for me seven days from now?"

When Harry did not reply, he went on: "I explained all this when you came to me for a loan, Harry. I can't make exceptions. My word is at stake here. I give what I promise, no questions asked. I expect others to do the same." He watched as Harry took in the familiar argument. After a minute or two, he went on:

"So you're telling me you can't come up with the money, right?" Harry nodded feebly. Joe strolled back to stand behind his desk.

"Truth is, Harry, you can do us both a favor," he said as he sat down. "Friends help one another, right? I helped you out of a tough spot, when no one else was around for you. But, you can't come up with the money you owe me. I don't like to think about what might happen, Harry. A deal is a deal. You know the rules. Everybody knows. We're here for you, but you gotta respect the rules. Right?" Harry did not reply. "So even if I could, which I can't, but even if I wait until next week, tell me Harry, where would you get the money to pay me next week? You see, Harry, you have no plan. You're desperate, That's no good. If there's no money coming to me, well, like I said, rules are rules. Even if I wanted to help you, I don't have the last word. My boss doesn't take excuses."

"I'll have the money by next week. I've got calls in."

Joe frowned. "Calls get you the answering machine. No, Harry, you've got to do better than that. Anyway, the bottom line is, I can't wait. I have others to think about. My cash flow depends on people respecting their obligations. I've got my own bills to pay. I don't get extensions any more than you do. Nothing personal. But in this business, Harry, we can't run to Judge Judy. You made a deal with us. We are the court, the judge and jury. You can't run to the police."

Harry looked genuinely shocked. "I'd never do that!"

"Nooooo, . . . you won't . . . What I'm saying here, Harry, is that you've got to make good on your loan today. Pay up now. Not tomorrow or next week. This afternoon, Harry. Before you go home."

Harry spread out his hands and shook his head. His whole body seemed to cave in where he sat. "I can't. I don't have it."

Joe looked across the room and addressed Bonz. "Hear that? He doesn't have the money." He got up again and circled slowly around Harry, returning to his desk again, after a few seconds, where he sat down and cupped his face in his hands. "He came today to tell me he can't pay me back."

Harry said miserably, "I just don't have it. I'm sorry Joe. I haven't slept for three nights thinking about it."

Joe sighed. Bonz shifted slightly where he stood.

"Well, now, Harry, you put me in a tough spot. I've helped you out before, but that was chicken feed compared to what you owe me this time. I'll have to tell the boss about it, and that's trouble. And you certainly don't want to get your wife involved — "

"Keep her out of it! She has nothing to do with this!" said Harry, jumping out of his chair and rubbing his hands nervously. Joe watched him for a few seconds then waved him down.

"Sit down, sit down." He waited for him to resume his seat. "Hey, I wouldn't want *my* wife to know either. And we want to keep it that way, right?" Harry nodded. He felt the pressure building up behind his eyes, suddenly tired, tense and nervous. "Sure we do. Believe me, I know how you feel. But it doesn't solve the problem, Harry. You know it. I know it."

"Take it out on me, if you have to," said the other man, with a touch of bravado. "just leave my family out of it." The words echoed emptily in the cavity of his head.

"Harry, Harry," said Joe softly, assuming a stricken look. "I don't want to hurt anybody. We can settle this, believe me." He waited a few seconds, then went on. "I helped you out of a tough spot, when no one else was around for you. I figure, given the circumstances, your not having the money to pay me today, and not likely to have it next week or the week after that, and with every passing day getting in deeper and deeper, making it tougher and tougher for me . . . ." He sighed as though it was too painful to finish the sentence. After a while, he went on. "Well, like I said, we can work something out." Harry said nothing. Joe pushed back his chair and crossed his legs.

"Here's the story, Harry. I need someone to do something for me. No big deal. You just do what Bonz tells you, in and out, nothing to think about, no snags. Easy as sucking on mother's milk. Everything is taken care of, from beginning to end, and you not only get your loan paid off, you get a bonus too. Fifteen big big ones." He let that sink in. Harry took a large breath. Joe had lit another cigarette but seemed to have forgotten it in the ashtray. Now he picked it up and puffed on it. "You'll be driven somewhere and driven back. No sweat. When you go home, you tell your wife you got lucky, you won big today. Don't worry, we'll give you the stubs, she'll believe you. She's been after you for a bigger house, right?"

Harry looked genuinely surprised. Joe laughed.

"Hey, we do our homework. We know everything about you. About Dotty, about your daughter Lisa, your brother Alphonse . . . ." Harry groaned where he sat. "I've gotta know who I'm doing business with, stands to reason." He watched Harry through narrowed eyes. He came around the desk to where Harry sat and bent down, bringing his face close to Harry's. "Well, you can do something about it with the money you'll get. It's more than enough for a down payment on that nice place in Riverdale she took you to see a couple of weeks ago." He straightened up slowly and went on: "Bonz is going to take you downtown, you do your thing and he drives you back here. Easy as pie. Not bad for less than an hour's work. Like Wheel of Fortune, right Bonz?" The big man laughed. It sounded like a growl.

"Somebody has done a terrible thing, Harry. He has to be punished. Well, there's a lot more to it, but I won't bore you with the details. Believe me, the last thing we want is to get anybody into trouble. But we have to protect our own. People like you. Loyal, respectful guys who know the rules and stick by them. That's why I'm asking you, Harry. I know I can trust you. We want to prove to you how much we respect you. We're giving you a job to do that settles everything between us. The loan. The interest. The penalty. Nobody outside this room will ever know about this conversation. You walk out of here through that door and come back directly into this room through the same door."

Harry turned to look where Joe had pointed but saw no door. He lowered his head as the other went on:

"Bonz drives you there. You do what he tells you. He drives you back here. After a while you leave up front, the way you came this morning. You get into your car that's been parked outside all the while, and you drive home." He paused but only for a moment. "Gina and five other people will see you leave. They saw you come in, they see you go out. They can all swear to it, if they have to, which believe me they won't have to."

Harry looked miserably at Joe, who walked back to his side of the desk and stood there, examining his nails.

Harry said: "What are you asking me to do?"

Joe asked, as though he had not heard Harry's question: "Did you tell your wife about the loan?"

"I didn't want to! But she can see right through me! She knows . . . . She knows I'm trying to get some money together to pay my debts."

"You owe her Harry. She deserves better."

"Don't you think I know that! Gambling is an addiction!"

The other man spoke softly. "I really hope you're wrong, Harry. Because I don't want this to happen again. And I don't want to see you get into bigger trouble."

"She'd kill me if she knew about it!"

"Then there's nothing to worry about. You will have had a good day. You won a big sum on a long shot, and tell her to keep it under wraps or the IRS will be on top of you and she'll get a lot of people into trouble, me, Bonz, all your friends who trusted you. And — are you listening, Harry?" Only when the other man nodded, did he continue " — and you give her that money for a down payment on the new house. Got that Harry? A house in her name. You paid what you owed me today, and you still had enough left for that, tell her. Got it?"

Harry did not answer. The pressure in his head had turned into a major headache. He saw Bonz move behind

Joe's desk and pressed a button. A framed print swung out to reveal the door of a safe. He watched as Bonz turned the knob several times and took from the safe, when it opened, a shoe box. He placed it carefully on the desk, then turned to close the safe. He tried the knob before approaching the desk again. Joe, standing beside him, had opened the box and with great care took out a small revolver.

"One of the best. Very efficient. All you do is aim and pull the trigger. You can't miss. Even without all those trophies you piled up before you decided to leave the force. A kid could do it. Bonz will explain everything on the way."

Harry jumped up from his seat as though a bolt of lightning had shot through him. "You're crazy! You know what you're asking me to do?" Bonz took a step forward as though to grab him, but Joe waved him off.

"You have a better idea, Harry? Tell me about it."

"Murder! You're asking me to murder someone I don't even know!"

"If you knew him, there would be a real problem. This way, well you're not involved, see?"

"What do you mean, I'm not involved? I'll be involved for the rest of my life!"

Joe seemed unmoved. "What if I told you, Harry, that no one, *not a single person connected with me*" — he tapped his finger on the desk with every word, spacing each one evenly, in a monotone, for emphasis — "*not a one* has ever been been arrested, or served jail time, period."

Harry looked first at Joe then at Bonz, the enormity of the situation stifling him. "Why me?" he asked feebly.

"Someone nobody knows, someone nobody can trace or identify. No motive. Oh, they always question *us*, we're the "usual suspects," as they say in that movie . . . ." he turned to Bonz, smiling, "what's the name of it, Bonz? I can never remember — "

"Casablanca," muttered Bonz, through tight lips.

"Yeah, that's it." He started to sing. "*'You must remember this, A kiss is still a kiss . . .'* yeah, a great movie — " He seemed lost in a reverie of his own for a few seconds.

"Remember. Gina and at least five other people out there, waiting to talk to me, saw you come in earlier and will see you leave through the same front door in about an hour. That's it. You've been with me until you leave to go home. I'll have the cash ready for you when you get back."

"I don't think I can do this, even if I wanted to. I *know* I can't do it!"

"Sure you can." He picked up the gun and turned it over again slowly, with exaggerated care. Bonz watched him closely, said in is thick hoarse voice:

"I took it apart a couple of hours ago. It's OK."

Joe nodded and handed the gun to Bonz, who replaced it in the box.

"It's business, Harry. Business. Just remember that and you'll be fine." He looked at his watch. "Let's see, it's twelve-thirty. You've been here since before noon. I'm gonna order lunch for all three of us in about fifteen minutes. Gina, my secretary will buzz me when the food comes. I take the food from her at the door. As far as she knows you guys are still with me in here, why else would I have ordered all that food?" He laughed before going on. "We're in here having a bite to eat, right, Bonz?" The big man answered with the usual low growl, his lips parting in a grimace. Then, as though a silent signal had been given, the large man picked up the box and went to where Joe had pointed earlier. There, he took out a small remote device from his pocket, pressed it and waited for a panel to open in the wall. He jerked his head, motioning Harry to follow him.

Harry took in the secret entrance, the box tucked under Bonz's left arm, Joe walking over to the opening and standing there, with his hands in his pockets, waiting for him to move out with Bonz. He tried to stand, fell back into his chair instead. With a tremendous effort, he stood up again, holding on to the arms of the chair for balance.

Even before he started to walk toward the open panel, Bonz had disappeared down the dark passageway. Harry followed. He heard the panel shut softly behind him. A glimmer of light some few hundred feet ahead told him the walk would not be a long one. Long or short, he knew there was no turning back. There had been no real choice, he told himself. And yet, he knew in his heart that a choice had been made and that he was indeed responsible for it. The truth of the knowledge gave him a strange release, a sense of peace, almost. Simultaneously, his adrenaline kicked in, a new burst of energy quickening his step. His mind had shed all arguments and doubts. Even his headache was gone.

As he followed Bonz to the end of the passage and into a small private yard, where a car was parked, he wondered at the change that had come over him in those few seconds since leaving Joe's office. He had accepted the inevitable, the realization that the only way to survive was to swim with the current, go through the motions that could buy time. Meanwhile, he would do what was asked and pull down the shutters of the soul.

Suddenly. as though it had happened yesterday, not eighteen years ago when he was a teenager, he heard again his kid brother asking him as they rode on the bus to school one morning:

"What's the difference between half a story and a third of the pie?" He'd shrugged, hiding his curiosity.

"What kind of crazy question is that?"

"Just answer it!"

"They're not the same! You can't compare them, you jerk!" He was eager to hear the answer but didn't want to let on. He frowned and asked: "What's the question again?" His brother rolled his eyes in mock exasperation:

"What's the difference between half a story and a third of the pie?"

"Which half of the story?"

"Awgeez! What's the difference?"

"Hey, if it's the second half, you can pretty well figure out the beginning, right? If it's the first half, you can't guess the ending!"

"So, take whichever half you like!"

"The second half. If you know how it turns out you can figure out the rest, right? And a third of the pie means you still have two more helpings the same size. So, no surprises. Is that it?"

He tried to recall what the punch line was but found he couldn't dredge it up. Why had that incident suddenly loomed up out of nowhere, after so many years?

As though on cue, he saw again Bonz's thick back as he led the way into the hidden passageway. A rush of fear flooded his stomach. The unbidden image slowly receded, but the earlier illusion of strength had dissipated. He saw vividly, as in a silent nightmare, what the future held for him. They had him trapped. He'd listened, gone along, he'd chosen to do what they wanted.

He couldn't stop gambling. The debts would pile up. Joe was counting on it, in spite of what he had said, all those friendly warnings about quitting, taking care of his wife. Even with the down payment they promised him, where was he going to get the rest of the money for a new place? A lot of bullshit! They had him by the short hairs.

The day had turned into a claustrophobic hell. He was reminded of Mr. Gorton, his English teacher at All Saints trying to explain Dante's *Inferno* to them, the rage and frustration of sinners who were able to see the future but knew at the same time that they would be trapped forever in their blind impotence when that future was closed off on the day of Judgment.

They had the ending to the story. But there would never be joy or pleasure in the knowledge of what was coming, in the clear vision of their poisoned future, closed off forever from light and hope, the rest of the pie.

He didn't have to wait for Hell. He saw with clarity the completed deed, felt the weight of it in the pit of his soul, a festering growth.

KALEIDOSCOPE

She should have gotten used to the idea after three weeks. But on this crisp April morning, outside the church of St. Stanislaus, Helen waited for the hearse to arrive, utterly convinced that it was all a mistake. She simply did not believe that Dick was dead, had been dead for almost a month, and that what was left of his body was in the sealed container about to arrive where she and two other of his long-time friends waited, outside the church.

The grief thrust upon her when the news came was all too real. But it was grief for Dick having chosen to make them *think* he was dead. Everything about him had been veiled in mystery; why should his dying be any different?

Another car had pulled up behind theirs. Helen recognized the new arrivals. They were, like herself, former Columbia graduate students who had first met Dick, as she and her husband had, in a sociology course. Two years later, Hal and Jenny had married, just around the time Jenny's cancer had first been diagnosed.

Fred Anderson nudged her and leaned close to say:

"I can't believe Hal brought Jenny out here today!" Helen watched as the grotesque figure, carefully bundled in a heavy jacket and a woolen blanket, was lifted up from the front seat and placed into the wheelchair her husband had taken from the trunk of the car. Fred quickly went forward to greet them. He helped Hal adjust the footrests on the chair then bent down to speak to Jenny. Hal said something to his wife as he started to wheel the chair toward Helen, Fred trailing behind. A small hat rested at a comic angle on Jenny's head — it had settled like that as a result of her being moved out of the car, lifted, set down in the wheelchair. The hat, the black patch over the left eye, where the most recent cancer had come to reside and where only the empty socket remained, together with her distorted mouth, gave her the appearance of a clown.

Jenny turned her scarred face toward Helen and said something. Helen nodded, not even trying to decipher the guttural sounds which passed as words ever since the removal of Jenny's larynx. Helen didn't have time or the will power to adjust to the sounds. She nodded helplessly, hoping that it was a proper response.

How long ago it seemed, all of them talking for hours over coffee or beer, before Jenny's cancer was first discovered at twenty-six! Before Fred married his cocktail waitress and moved to New Jersey, determined to be happy and succeeding — against all predictions — in raising a perfectly ordinary nice middle-class family! Before Dick so cruelly dropped out of their lives!

Yet, it *was* death that rode up to the tiny cluster of people standing in front of the church and came to a halt in front of the entrance, where a spot had been kept open for the hearse. An odor of decay tainted the April sunlight like a spreading stain. Incredulity and dismay churned inside her, then fear surfaced, like bad breath.

Someone tugged at her sleeve. It was Fred. Helen did not recognize the woman beside him.

"I don't think you've ever met Laura Platzek. And this is her husband, Stan Platzek." A thin balding man held out his hand. Helen took it, murmured something. Mrs. Platzek acknowledged the introduction with a slight nod as she blew her nose, red and swollen from weeping. Helen had heard all about her from Fred, everybody knew the story about Dick's "wife," the Polish woman he'd married, brought to the States, and promptly divorced, once she was established as a citizen. The woman with whom he had never lived, with whom an understanding had been made and honored. It all made sense, of course; but why then was the woman crying like that? It seemed excessive.

For Helen, Laura Platzek had never really existed until this moment. Dick himself had never mentioned her; but Fred had shared bits and pieces of the story over the years. During their Columbia days, Dick had spent more time with Fred than with any of his other friends and apparently had told him a good deal about his past life. She felt a twinge of resentment (envy?) at Fred's knowing more than she did about that marriage, about this plain woman, now called Laura Platzek, who had been so close to Dick for a time . . . . Did she share secrets of a special kind? Had they in fact been lovers? If not, why all those tears, her husband standing there, right beside her?

She caught herself sharply. What was she thinking! They all knew how Dick had helped the woman get out of the country, make a new life for herself. He had simply come to her rescue. There was nothing more to it!

A commotion by the church entrance jolted her into awareness. The priest had come out in his vestments and was carrying on an animated conversation with the undertaker. The back door of the hearse was now open; the container visible inside. The Platzeks and Fred had gone over to join the priest and Mr. Russell, the mortician.

A cab drew up. Helen recognized Steve Besorian and Dr. Hadad, two of Dick's oldest friends. Even before the car had come to a halt, Steve had the door open and was crossing over to the small group clustered near the entrance to the church. Dr. Hadad paid the driver and joined Helen. Steve left the others and came over to them.

"I knew it, I told you there would be trouble!" he began by way of greeting. There was a stubborn petulance about him, but even his deep frown did not detract from his Armenian good looks: thick almost black hair, a long straight nose, and eyes that bored through you, held you, and would not let go. He was well aware of the impression he created and made the most of it.

"What do you mean, what trouble?" Helen asked.

Frowning and restless where he stood, Steve replied angrily: "Something about health regulations! The crate can't be taken into the church!"

"But those people — " she gestured in the direction of the Platzeks — "expect a Mass." Fred came up to them and said, in a conspiratorial whisper:

"Father Domboski has gone inside to change!"

Steve frowned. "So, that's *it*?"

Mr. Russell walked over and told them to get back into the car, the procession was ready to move out. He confirmed what they had just learned.

"No Mass?" Helen asked.

Before anyone could answer, Steve pointed to the Platzeks, who were getting into their car. "Doesn't she have a say in this?"

Fred shook his head, took Helen's arm and steered her to their car. The priest had emerged in his street clothes and now climbed into the Platzeks' car. The hearse began to pull away from the curb; the Platzeks's car followed. Fred waited for Helen to settle in the back seat, near the window, then took his place up front next to the driver, a friend of Dick's she vaguely remembered meeting at some lecture.

Dr. Hadad reached across Steve, who was sitting in the middle, and touched Helen's arm.

"How is your husband?"

"He still has a touch of the flu."

For a while no one spoke. They cleared the curb and positioned themselves behind the Platzeks's. As the three-car procession headed for the Expressway, Fred squirmed around to address those in the back. His voice was unnaturally loud in the confines of the car. He was deaf in one ear.

"Too bad about the Mass," he said.

"I mean, will somebody explain it to me?" Steve blurted out in a sudden release of words and pent-up emotion. "The crate was hermetically sealed! Why should there be a problem?" When no one volunteered an answer, he crossed his arms over his chest, his frustration eloquent in his rigid posture. The man at the wheel glanced at him in the mirror and said: "Something about the paper work."

Fred suddenly seemed to remember he had not introduced the driver. "This is Bod Janoswki, an old friend of Dick's from New Jersey. He offered to drive me and pick up Helen on the way. His wife is visiting with her mother for a week, and he has plenty of time on his hands, right?" He jabbed his friend with his elbow. They both laughed at some private joke.

Steve said: "Don't do that. He's driving."

"There *are* health department rulings, papers have to be in order," Dr. Hadad volunteered, leaning forward so Fred, as well as the others, could hear him.

She felt a stirring in the pit of her stomach, a pressure behind her eyes, the same sensation she had experienced on that morning, three weeks earlier, when Fred had telephoned to tell them that Dick had died in Marseilles of a heart attack.

She flinched again now, as she had then, recalling the familiar combination of surprise and grief in her husband's voice. She had jumped to the conclusion that the call was about Jenny. Wasn't she the most likely candidate? Had they found another cancer? But her husband had put down the phone and told her Dick was dead.

At first, a cold wave of guilt swept over her for having so quickly assumed it had been Jenny and — worse still — for having felt no emotion at all. Then a blanket of stifling despair threatened to suffocate her as the news forced its way through the protective layers of her disbelief. He was due back in New York in a matter of days. They were all looking forward to it; he'd been gone almost a year, the longest absence yet. Instead, the same merchant ship on which he had signed up a year ago had brought home the "remains." Or so they were told. Where had he been? If only she had asked more questions before he left. Now, no one would ever know what he had been doing, where he had been, where he had disappeared, this time cutting them all off completely —

She searched her memories for some clues.

With his Columbia friends, he lived in an eternal present. He would drop in casually to see Helen and her husband — they were only a few blocks away — for long chats, lots of coffee and wine, sometimes a game of cards. Then suddenly he was off again: Peru, Brazil, Colombia, Panama, Russia, Norway, New Zealand, Taiwan. This last trip had been the longest. "I should be back by April," he had said when he visited them the evening before his ship sailed. And all through that cold February and March, she had warmed herself with the thought that he would soon be with them again.

Lost in her reverie, she didn't hear Fred addressing her. He leaned back and touched her knee tentatively.

"Are you comfortable there?"

"I'm fine," she said, turning briefly to acknowledge his attention with a small smile, then burrowed deeper into her corner and stared out the car window, her head resting against the glass. Fred was pleasant enough, so long as he didn't get on to pornography or dirty jokes. He enjoyed recounting escapades that even a Titan would have blushed to claim. Once, Steve had scolded him for talking about his wife and her prowess in bed. Steve was quirky in his own way, but he was inflexible when it came to propriety and was outspoken in criticizing dirty talk. But in spite of what even her husband considered to be a major failing in Fred (he had put him down once when Fred had indulged in describing a torrid weekend with one of his girlfriends), Helen preferred him to Steve, who was often moody, prissy even, difficult to read.

"Remember to keep in line," Steve was saying to Bod. "The cars can go through red lights so long as they're following the hearse." They were last in the procession. "And you'd better turn on your lights." They were on the Expressway now, heading toward Long Island.

"The only way would have been to open the crate, but the legal formalities are just too difficult," Dr. Hadad was saying, in answer to some question Helen had missed.

"Well, why the hell didn't she take care of it! At least we would have been sure!" said Steve.

"Oh, don't start again!" said Fred with an edge to his voice. "We went all through that last night, how many times? Why are you still bringing it up!"

"I hadn't seen that damn crate then!"

Dr. Hadad tried to smooth things over. "The poor woman has had enough on her mind. When you consider, she really didn't have to take on this burden. She's not related to him . . . . Try putting yourself in her place. She's had a real husband and family for almost ten years now. Dick went out of his way to help her back then. Sure he changed her life, she knows that better than any of us. But she wasn't bound legally or in any other way to take on the funeral arrangements."

"It was the least she could do, bury him!" was the sharp retort. "You just said, Dick changed her life. She owes him that, at least! Anyway, what arrangements! She didn't even plan a small lunch for his old friends. What kind of funeral is that?"

"You've got a big mouth, you know that? Never know when to stop! Petty! Worse than a woman!" Fred said angrily, at the same time that Dr. Hadad had started to speak, his words softening the effect of Fred's harsh comment.

"You're being too hard on her, Steve. She really is under no obligation. What happened back then was a favor. Past history. She didn't have to bury him. It's not as though she had ever really been his wife!"

"And how do you think she felt," Fred chimed in, following his own track, "getting a long distance call from some stranger in Marseilles who tells her that Dick had suddenly dropped dead?"

"Well, she was down as next of kin. Not his sister, mind you," Steve went on, taking in greedily the effect of his words. Helen looked up sharply; Fred shook his head and threw up his hands; Dr. Hadad leaned forward and said, in his even, patient voice. "Believe me, it was just a formality. I still say, she was under no obligation. She could have stayed home today and just had him buried by the undertaker."

Steve suddenly was furious. "What the hell are you talking about!" he shouted in his clear diction, each word spaced out with careful deliberation. He had been an actor, briefly, and still dreamed of a stage career. "She damn well had an obligation! Aside from all that he did to get her out of Poland, he left her everything, she's his *heir!*"

There was an embarrassed silence. Steve seemed to have been energized by the fall-out his words produced and went on in his strong voice: "Bottom line is, she *owes* him! He saved her from God knows what, I never asked and he never said, but it must have been pretty awful! And she's been in the picture ever since!"

Fred had recovered himself enough not to sound angry this time. "You don't know anything about their relationship! Even if she has been in the picture all this time, which isn't true, mind you, who are you to decide she has to play by your rules?" He shook his head.

"I think what Steve meant," said Dr. Hadad in his reassuring voice, "is, whoever was authorized to take care of the formalities should have made sure that the papers were properly filed. Identification at this end could have been – "

Steve jumped in. "See? *Somebody* understands!" But before he could continue, Dr. Hadad leaned toward him and said quickly:

"But, Steve, I don't think it would have been wise to open the crate."

"Why not?" asked Steve, pursing his mouth to match a deep frown of disapproval.

"Many reasons," replied the doctor.

"What about the sister in Poland? Shouldn't she have been notified, asked about the arrangements?" Steve persisted.

"Oh she was notified," offered Bod, unexpectedly.

"The point is," Steve went on with characteristic doggedness, "everything is wrong. No Mass. We're told to go directly to the cemetery. What kind of funeral is this?"

Fred said placatingly. "O.K. So maybe Laura missed something. She did the best she could."

Steve tried a new tack. "Jesus!! To find out at the last minute, with the priest ready to take the coffin into the church, that the paper work was not properly filed! Maybe that's why she's crying her eyes out!"

"It's over, finished," said Bod over his shoulder, suddenly annoyed. He obviously hadn't missed a word. "You don't have to insult the poor woman!"

Fred said: "Keep your eyes on the road."

"I'm not insulting anybody. If anything, *I'm* the one who's been insulted! Don't you think there should at least have been a blessing in the vestibule? Time for us to go inside and say a prayer?"

"Oh, cut it out!" Fred said in a loud voice, clearly exasperated. "You ramble like an old nag! Never satisfied!"

Steve leaned forward until he was almost level with Fred's good ear. "Let me tell you what *I* think, friend! I think the whole business is weird. If you ask me," he went on, settling back in his seat, ready to launch into some kind of revelation, "if you want to know what I *really* think —"

"Save it," interrupted Fred with asperity.

"I'm *not* satisfied, you're right about that! Dick was perfectly healthy. A man like that doesn't fall down dead at thirty-nine." He waited, letting it sink in. "You've wondered too. Don't deny it. Everybody has."

Fred sighed. "We've been all through that. Let up, will you? We'll never have all the facts. The one fact that matters is right there, riding in front of us." He pointed to the hearse.

"*What* fact? That *crate*? Who the hell knows what's inside? For all we know it could be oranges or grapefruits!"

The eloquent silence that followed startled even Steve into some measure of caution. It was Dr. Hadad who picked up the thread, in his placid tone:

"There was an official autopsy in Marseilles."

"But no one actually identified the body at this end, right?" Steve had simmered down a bit but clearly was not ready to let go.

Once again, Dr. Hadad seemed to sense Steve's need for reassurance. He spoke calmly, deliberately, in contrast to Steve's jagged questions. "There was no need to. The captain had identified the body in Marseilles."

Steve did not answer Dr. Hadad but leaned forward instead and spoke into Fred's good ear, loud enough for the others to make out the words. "What came back are *remains*! Literally. *Parts* of the body." He pointed to Dr.

Hadad, sitting beside him. "You told me yourself, the other night, after you made those calls — "

Fred shifted in his seat. Helen frowned. Hadad said quickly: "It was just a rumour — "

"Why couldn't they have shipped him in a regular casket, *whatever* was inside," Steve interrupted. "For the sake of appearances, at least."

"God, if I'd known he would carry on like this," said Fred, raising his eyes toward some heaven close by, "I would have bought a silver one, paid for it myself."

"This conversation isn't going anywhere," said Dr. Hadad in a low voice, glancing at Helen, who had closed her eyes. "I, for one, don't play guessing games. And that's what this is, all this talk."

Steve said, pointing to the hearse up ahead: "And I, for one, don't think it's Dick up there, in that hearse, what do you think of that?"

Fred turned around impatiently, ready with a reply, but the doctor reached out and touched his arm, glancing at Helen as he did so.

"That's nonsense, Steve, and you know it," said the doctor. "It doesn't help any to indulge in fantasies."

"He's dead all right," said Fred.

The words bounced off Helen's consciousness, her heart lurching with the sudden unwelcome realization that she had been deluding herself all along. The certainty she had nurtured all those weeks now shattered into shards of discarded hope. There was no longer any doubt in her mind. Death was riding up ahead, in an unfinished wooden container. Not Dick's big body, but his *remains*; literally, those *parts* of the body that were left, whatever the reason for the mutilation. For there had been mutilation, she was sure of it. She wondered briefly how or why she had reached that unexpected conclusion, how she could accept it so easily, without craving any further explanations.

Dr. Hadad had reached across Steve to touch her arm. As she opened her eyes, he smiled and asked: "Are you all right?"

"Yes, fine." She sat up and pushed back her hair. "How much longer?"

"A few more minutes," said Bod.

They were nearing the exit ramp. Another funeral, a long procession, was directly in front of theirs. A third one followed their cortège. Helen had a moment of panic, a kind of claustrophobic attack that took her breath away. When she was very young, driving in a car, she would hang on to whoever was close by when they sped over a bump. She felt at those times that she was falling from a high place. She felt that now and leaned forward automatically, clutching the top of the seat directly in front of her. Bod felt the movement and turned slightly to look back at her in the rear view mirror.

"Sorry."

"We were just saying — " Steve began, but Helen interrupted him.

"I know," she said in a rush, suddenly eager to share her thoughts and feelings. It was as though floodgates had been opened and all her questions had cascaded out to find their level and come to rest, not in answers but in a single unruffled truth. "He led a strange life, didn't he? We'd get postcards from all over the world, but he wasn't just traveling, was he? He gave the impression he was on assignment. We were sure he was in the secret service. Did you think that too? Was it you, Fred, who told us he had three passports? And the time he went to India, he — " She turned to Steve and Dr. Hadad, sitting on her left. Both men were staring at her. "I'm sorry. I've been rattling on."

"We've all wondered what he was up to, said Steve, suddenly deflated. Dr. Hadad reached across him once more, this time to hold Helen's hand as he spoke.

"Of course, we've all wondered where he went, what he did. It was a strange life, you're right. But we never asked him about it when he was alive. Should we be dredging it all up now, when he's dead?"

"I always suspected he was an undercover agent," Helen went on, repeating what she had often thought, as though exorcising one last demon inside her. She moved slightly where she sat. Dr. Hadad released her hand and pulled away.

"And, if he was?" he asked, looking straight ahead.

"Well, it would explain a hell of a lot, is what Helen is trying to say!" volunteered Steve.

"This speculating is . . . unhealthy," said Dr. Hadad.

"You're right," said Fred. "We shouldn't pry."

"Well, you know, that crate could be the perfect screen for whatever may be going on," said Steve with renewed vigor. "Listen, humor me for a minute, okay? Suppose he — " But Hadad interrupted.

"Suppose you change the subject, Steve," he said in a peremptory tone that was out of character. "Let's not open up a Pandora's box. There's no point to it. It might be dangerous, too, if everything you're suggesting is true."

There was a certain urgency in the doctor's tone. Helen wondered, could Hadad be monitoring them all? Could he know something about Dick's death that he could not or would not share with them? He was Dick's oldest friend. They had known each other (or so she had been told) for over fifteen years. They had met somewhere in Europe, both in their early twenties. Had the meeting really been an accident; what followed, pure coincidence? Or were they both involved from the very beginning in some secret activity, protecting one another along the way? Was Hadad still protecting Dick, even now trying to bury whatever truth lay behind his friend's strange death?

" . . . foul play," Steve was saying.

"We'll never know. Dr. Hadad is absolutely right," said Fred. "Let's drop it." But, this time, for some reason, Dr. Hadad was eager to continue.

"If Dick was an agent, let's just suppose that — and I'm not saying I go along with such a notion for a minute! — do you think our raising dust like this will help?"

Yes, Helen thought, *but not for the reason you think.* Dick was dead, but it was suddenly imperative to recall the life he had shared with them, to interpret in a new light his stories of adventures back in Poland as a boy, later as an adult (but when did he go back, and why?); in Chile once, when a dog saved his life during an earthquake, pulling him away from a high promontory just as the earth cracked and a rift appeared a few feet away where he had been resting under a tree; as a seaman on British cargo ships; searching for Norwegian nationals who had taken refuge in South America . . . . And those passports!

" . . . and if he *has* gone under cover," Fred was saying, "he wouldn't want you to find him, would he?!"

Had she been in love with him? Was that the reason for this compelling need to gather together the scattered facts about him? To shape a life for him out of those bits and pieces of information they all shared? To be able to nurture some sort of memory instead of a mystery? Could they ever have become lovers? Had she been older, more experienced, would she have given him some sign? Would he have responded? Or would he have remained immune, like the great god Pan, whose magic chords drew others to him, the source of love but also of the despair attending its frustrated potential?

Steve and Fred had lapsed into a low-key exchange. The cars had left the highway and were now on a local road. The cemetery was just ahead. Steve was saying:

" . . . he was in our seminar, remember? Dick had borrowed some money from him, oh years ago — God knows for what, for Laura maybe or for his sister back in Poland — and just before he left last year he went out to see him, in New Jersey, and paid him back."

"He said when he left that he was going to finish up his degree this Fall," said Fred.

"I think he meant it," said Steve. "He actually wrote three term papers just before he left." Helen had helped him with two of the papers, . . . but why did he suddenly want to finish up? In the years they had known him, he must have accumulated more than enough credits for a degree, but he had always audited whatever he fancied, foregoing grades. A degree meant formal requirements, in addition to a sequence of courses and letter grades. It meant periodic meetings with a mentor, a comprehensive exam, a dissertation, finally, and then a defense of it — the kind of focus and timetable Dick could not possibly have maintained, given his abrupt comings and goings. As a "special student," he had remained in the shadows of the academic arena, giving out very little about himself. Such had been his preference. Had all that changed? To Helen, Steve's conclusion didn't make sense. Out loud she said:

"But he knew he could never do all the things a degree calls for. Think about it. No, there has to be some other explanation . . . . Even if he's gone under cover, he certainly can't come back to finish his degree here. Not even with a new face, a new identity, new everything."

"We'd never recognize him, that's for sure!" said Fred. "He could be alive this very minute, watching us from out there, knowing — "

" — knowing we don't want him to be dead," Steve interrupted, glancing at Dr. Hadad as though expecting him to say something. But it was Fred who picked it up.

"Dead but not really dead?"

"No, he's really dead," said Helen, unable to stop herself. All but Bod turned to look at her. She felt them appraising her in a new way. She went on. "It helps to think that he had to disappear, but, I don't believe that." She brought out the last words with difficulty. The catch in her throat made her think of Pearl, the clerk in the library, who had read so much in his affable greetings, his simple courtesies. A few times he had taken the shy girl for coffee at the nearby Chock Full O' Nuts, on the corner of Broadway. What would Pearl say when she learned he was never coming back?

The urge to lay out before them what she had been thinking, her feelings as they surfaced, was an imperative need. "He would never have agreed to disappear, for whatever reason, without giving us some sign." She took a deep breath then went on. "I think he was killed." The others stared at her, except Bod, who kept his eyes straight ahead, after a surreptitious glance in the rear-view mirror.

They were inside the cemetery gates, now. The hearse slowed down and came to a stop in front of the office. They all watched as Mr. Russell went inside. In a few minutes he was out again, and the cortège continued down a curving path to where a canopy marked the open grave. The mortician came over to their car, poked his head in the window that Fred had rolled down, and said:

"Please stay inside until the coffin has been carried to the site. I'll signal you when we're ready."

They all watched as the wooden box was taken out of the hearse and carried to the newly-dug hole. At the signal, they all got out and moved across the thin grass to the place where Father Domboski already had positioned himself. As the priest was coming to the end of his prayers, the mortician handed each of them a white rosebud with instructions to drop it with a "last goodbye" on top of the crate. It was all over in a mater of minutes.

To Helen, the service was in every way inadequate. The priest was obviously ill at ease, there was a general air of unresolved expectancy among the others standing by the open grave. She hurried back to the car and settled herself inside, without saying goodbye to Jenny or the Platzeks. The empty hearse worked its way around the parked cars and picked up speed as it moved away. Fred and Steve, deep in conversation, strolled back and stood waiting for Bod and the doctor to catch up before getting in. They all watched in silence as the car with the priest and the Platzeks eased into the roadway and moved toward the cemetery gate. Laura Platzek rode with her husband, in the back, her face a pale pinched mask.

On the Expressway again, the men debated about where to have lunch. They finally decided on Sloppy Louie's on Fulton Street, and after some coaxing Helen agreed to join them instead of taking a cab home. It was almost three, the place was empty. A waiter was sprinkling sawdust on the bare floor. After taking the manager aside and putting some bills into his hand, Fred came back and sat down. "No problem," he reported, with a big smile.

The food, she remembered afterwards, was very good — but she couldn't remember what exactly she had ordered. The only vivid memory of that afternoon was Fred singing Cole Porter songs and Dr. Hadad telling them about the dangers of raw fish, as Steve, unperturbed, ate with relish his large platter of *sushi*.

Over coffee they reminisced about their Columbia days, how Dick used to bait them about their idol, an anthropologist who liked to reduce all social phenomena to "X" and "Y" equations. Sharing those memories seemed to relieve the tensions that had built up earlier in the day. They were all in a good mood by the time they reached Helen's place. Dr. Hadad walked her to the entrance.

"So long as we act as though we're masters of our destiny, nothing is worth brooding about." He kissed the back of her hand. "We're not, of course," he added with a smile. "But you know that." She nodded, not altogether sure she understood the relevance of his words. No matter, she thought. It would keep for later.

Inside the apartment, she looked in on her sleeping husband. The covers were in disarray, but his face was no longer flushed. In the living room she picked up a brass Indian dish, Dick's last present. It was badly tarnished. She took it into the kitchen, put on plastic gloves, and cleaned it with Noxon, repeating the process several times, until the plate gleamed like gold. The simple chore seemed to wipe away all traces of the kaleidoscopic shifting emotions that had threatened to overwhelm her earlier that day.

Dick's last visit came back to her then. The TV had been left on, the volume low, and Helen had been glancing at the screen from time to time, where an episode of a popular TV series was going on. She heard someone ask: *Shouldn't a man like Colombo be more at home on a boat?* It struck her as a very funny line and she burst out laughing. She had shut off the TV then and listened while the two men launched into a discussion about ships, navigational instruments, maps and charts. They ended the evening with what had become a competitive sport: quoting from favorite poems, essays, and speeches.

After they had all contributed some Gilbert and Sullivan, Dick volunteered a piece of his own. "It's called 'Savage Poem'," he said, and then in his strong baritone — raised to a dramatic level for the occasion — recited:

> "One wife?
> Man —
> You gotta be kidding!
> Dat's like da monkies."

Her husband had objected that it was too short a piece to qualify as anything. Helen herself had observed irrelevantly — they had all been drinking wine since early afternoon — "Monkeys don't go to marriage counselors."

"Monkeys don't write books about it, either," her husband had added.

"Maybe monkeys are smarter than we are," Dick had answered. "Maybe they've put a ban on writing books. Far too many in print!" Her husband held up his hand in a commanding gesture.

"All right, wise guy!" he said to Dick. "Let's see you beat this one!" — and cleared his throat a few times before going on. It was a poem he had written while in the Air Force, one of Helen's favorites. "It should be sung to the tune of 'Paddy Mack who drove a hack'," he explained. He cleared his throat one more time. "The title is 'Where do we go from here?' " He took a few more seconds to settle back in his chair and assume a theatrical pose. "Are you ready?" Helen, her head to one side, nodded vigorously, trying not to giggle. Dick had sighed, crossed his arms and sat back with a look of resignation. Her husband glared at both of them, forcing them to full attention. Helen was familiar with the look. It was meant to forestall any interruption or criticism. When he was satisfied, he began half reciting, half singing to the tune he had mentioned earlier, with a strained concentration that transformed his face into a parody of Placido Domingo delivering a great operatic *aria*:

> *They asked the navigator*
> *"Where do we go from here?*
> *We'd like to have the heading*
> *And the time that we'll get there."*
>
> *The navigator looked above*
> *But couldn't find a star:*
> *"I can't say where I'm going . . . f o o r r–*
> *I don't know where we are!"*
>
> *The navigator found himself*
> *Surrounded by the crew:*

He reached for his computer
For he knew not what to do –

He quickly added altitude
The time and temperature,
Divided by the azimuth
And multiplied by four.

He wrote the answer in his log
Then turned to face the crew;
He raised an eyebrow very high
And said: "Here's what we'll do:

We'll take a bearing on a wave
And on a school of fish,
Move one line up and have a fix
As good as you could wish!"

The pilot threw the flying stick
The bombardier the sight;
The gunner seized him by the throat
And squeezed with all his might – !

And when they had the navigator
Pinned down on the floor,
Again they asked the quesh-tee-unnn . . .
That they had asked befooorrre – !
"OOhh, where do we go from here, man,
Where do we go from here?"

She found herself smiling. What was it Dick had said afterwards, trying to gain back the advantage? "Wit, my friend, is the lowest of the arts . . . . "

She stood in the deepening dusk, relishing the memory. In the bedroom, her husband stirred and called out to her. She moved quickly across the kitchen and went to him.

LAYOVER

The closing of the front door woke her. In the fuzzy semi-consciousness of the moment, she fought against the intrusion, lingered on the threshold of sleep. At the same time, a trace of anxiety insinuated itself into her familiar surroundings. She opened her eyes. A gray pencil-line of light where the drapes met told her it was almost dawn. Still fighting the urge to fall back into sleep, Linda groped for her wristwatch on the night table and peered at the luminous dials. Five minutes to seven.

Tom! Of course. Her brother Tom was with her. She sat up, fully awake now. He'd shown up with a girl two nights ago. Just as demanding as ever in his deceptively easy-going way. He was her brother, but over the past several years he had become a stranger.

When they arrived unexpectedly around midnight, her irritation must has shown, because he'd laughed and patted her shoulder as he swept past her into the tiny foyer and put down their three bags. "Relax, relax! It's only for a few days." But Linda knew that a few days for Tom could stretch into weeks, months even. He showed up only when he was broke or anticipating what he called "important shifts." What were sisters for?

She'd warned him the last time that she wouldn't take him in again. But it had been so late (on purpose?), she had no choice. "Don't fuss so much," he'd said. "Go about your business as though I'm a ghost." Sure . . . . Well, today she would tell him he, they, had to leave.

Even as her resolution hardened, she knew she would have to give him some money, for food at least. She was rarely home for meals, these days. The refrigerator was empty. She usually had a cup of coffee at work, a quick sandwich at her desk at lunchtime, and, for several months now, dinner with Victor in some modest restaurant.

And she'd have to give him a set of keys — the last thing she wanted to do, since she could no longer trust her brother.

She had trusted and loved him once, had taken care of him — and her father — when her mother began to show signs of the acute depression that finally forced them to place her in a nursing home. Tom was eight at the time, Linda thirteen. Often, hurrying through homework in the afternoon, so that she could start peeling vegetables for dinner and set the table, Linda would catch Mrs. Watkins, her mother's all-day nurse, watching her with something like pity in her eyes. Linda herself never questioned her role or complained. Who else was there to take care of Tom and her father?

Once she overheard Aunt Rudie, her father's sister, telling Daddy that he had spoiled Tom. Aunt Rudie and her husband Lenny had come from Oklahoma City, as they did every Spring for two weeks, ever since Mrs. Goodman had been put away. Aunt Rudie would air mattresses, sort out closets, buy them all new pajamas, shirts, shoes, while Uncle Lenny repaired appliances, checked lighting fixtures, built shelves, once even put down a flagstone patio. On this occasion, Aunt Rudie was preparing supper, Daddy and Uncle Lenny were sitting at the kitchen table sipping beer. "He should visit his mother more often, give Linda a break once in a while!" her aunt was saying. "I don't want to pressure the boy, he's had a rough time," Daddy had replied. "Boy! He's fifteen!" said Aunt Rudie. "I want him to finish school without distractions," her father had replied. "Linda finished school, didn't she, and she had more than her share of distractions!" her aunt had answered. "Never heard *her* complain. But that's no reason to take her for granted," "Now, Rudie," her uncle Lenny had interjected, don't be hard on your brother, he's got enough worries." "What he should worry about," his wife had persisted, "is that boy, lounging around all day, or disappearing for hours and turning up only to eat. You've spoiled him Henry."

Linda was twenty-two when her father died of a heart attack. She inherited the house, his bank account, his insurance, everything. Her father had told her years earlier that he would leave everything in her name so she could take care of her mother. She had put all the cash, what came in from the sale of the house and from the insurance policies into a special account with Aunt Rudie, for that purpose. There wasn't much left over, but by then she had a job, had seen her brother graduate from high school and had offered to send him on to college too, but Tom, more restless than ever, chose to leave home and look for work on the west coast. He liked working with his hands, he told her. And he obviously wanted to be on his own. Linda had supported him in the decision, although at the time she didn't like to see him go. She gave him five thousand dollars to tide him over until he found work. Periodically he would send a card, a new address; she wired him money whenever he asked for it.

Then, three years ago he suddenly began to drop in out of the blue. At first Linda took it in stride, but she grew increasingly annoyed at his suddenly turning up like that. It was always an emergency, it seemed, and Linda's questions always went unanswered. His reason for coming, though, was always predictably the same: he was out of a job and desperate for money. He never went into details.

What crisis had brought him back this time? The presence of the girl bothered Linda. The Tom she knew had never let anyone get close to him. And this girl was much like Tom himself, undemonstrative, moody. She doubted if Tom had brought her along just for sex. He knew, even as a teenager, how to get it without any trouble.

She couldn't, wouldn't take them in. She had plans and her erratic brother had no place in them, not any more. A new job and more money had enabled her to move into the two-bedroom brownstone apartment. Earlier in the year, with a brand new Associate degree in business administration from Borough of Manhattan Community College, she had applied for a managerial opening in the accounting firm where she worked and had been chosen for the job. She had settled into her new position with quiet efficiency. Her fellow workers liked and respected her; and although she didn't encourage friendships, she was always ready to listen to their problems, give advice. Her co-workers appreciated her interest. The only time she waved them away was when they tried to suggest a brighter wardrobe, more makeup, a new hairdo. She would laugh and shake her head. "I'll think about it," she would say.

It came as a surprise, therefore, when she suddenly started to spruce up and, after work one day, was seen meeting a man in the lobby of the building where she worked. It was Mrs. Carstairs from the steno pool who told the others the next morning. "A nice-looking guy, tall, blondish, well-dressed too. He took her arm and they walked out as though they'd been married for years." Linda herself said nothing to anyone. When Regina Foster, who was in the office next door, suggested one day that if she wanted to leave early some afternoon, she, Regina, would be happy to cover for her, Linda was genuinely surprised. "Why would I want to do that?" she asked.

As always, when not expected and not sought, love came as an earth-shaking blast with devastating aftershocks. Unprepared for it, Linda could only wonder at the changes it wrought in her. The vague stirrings she felt made her restless. This new kind of love was an alien concept to her, different from what she had felt for her family. For a while she felt uneasy, unsettled, her familiar routines slipping out of control. All she knew was that the agony and insecurity of those new emotions were in some way also very pleasant.

Victor Larsen too was a loner. For six years he had worked on cargo ships to the orient and South America. Back from a long trip to Chile, he had suddenly decided he'd had enough of the sea and took a job in a travel agency. Whether Victor felt the same unfamiliar stirrings Linda was experiencing, the same unsettling attraction, was not clear. The word *love* had never actually been used by either of them.

They'd met at a lecture on the Intrepid. At the reception later, they struck up an easy conversation and discovered they had many interests in common, especially their love of old books and watching the Antiques Road Show. They soon discovered other things in common: self-confidence, self-reliance, having to take care of themselves from an early age. Soon they become inseparable.

Tom's sudden appearance threatened to disrupt Linda's new personal schedule. For several weeks now, she had been meeting Victor after work for a modest early dinner, followed by a local concert or lecture, sometimes a movie. If Tom didn't leave in the morning, she would have to give him money for food and leave him a set of keys, something she wanted desperately to avoid doing. The alternative — not seeing Victor — was not an option.

The night they arrived, she followed them into the living room with apprehension. Her silence didn't bother Tom, or the girl for that matter. They seemed to expect resistance on her part. Her brother had gone straight to the small cupboard where she kept a quart of gin and a quart of scotch and had poured himself a generous measure of Dewars. He held up the glass to the girl, who shook her head. Sitting with his legs crossed on Linda's tweed sofa, he looked at his sister over the rim of his glass:

"We're off to New Zealand."

"Whatever for?" she asked, genuinely surprised.

"Work. What else?"

"Good lord. All the way there for a job?"

"A job's a job."

"What kind of job?"

"Assistant caretaker at one of the national parks."

"Are you qualified for that kind of work?"

"They think so."

"But, why there? Why not here?"

"Because this one was available. Besides, we like to travel, don't we, Bess." The girl said nothing.

"It's the other side of the world."

"It's a break."

"Not exactly an offer to take over the Wellington Branch of Citibank."

Tom scratched his ear. "Do they have a branch in Wellington?" When no one responded to his grin, he took a large gulp of the whiskey and went on: "This is a job where I can be my own man, out in the open, good conditions, free from the usual nine to five routines, you know?" He turned to Bess, who sat next to him, as if for confirmation. She looked at her toes and said nothing. "It's a change. And the money's good."

"But why would they want you instead of someone already there, one of their own, with experience in that kind of work?" Tom had shrugged, had not answered. "Are they paying your airfare?"

"Of course."

As if on cue, the girl said: "They're advancing him the money for the tickets."

"But you'll have to pay it back from your wages. Suppose you decide not to stay?"

"Why would I want to do that?" Your past record, she thought bitterly. Instead she found herself saying:

"But this is your country."

He'd gotten up then, a touch of impatience in his movements, and refilled his glass. Linda watched the level in the bottle go down to a third of capacity. Bess was watching him too. She tossed her hair back in a nervous gesture, on the brink of speaking, then relaxed on the sofa. Tom tasted his new drink, his back to them:

"More your country than mine, he said." There was a long silence. Outside a bus changed gears and moved away. Linda felt helpless. He seemed to read her thoughts, and when he spoke again it was as though he were the older one, reassuring his younger sibling.

"Relax, Sis. It's only a few days."

"Ten days," said Bess, almost defiantly.

"O.K. Ten days." He did not hide his impatience with the girl. He went to sit in the armchair by the window, putting distance between them.

"But I can't keep you here that long, Tom! I'm in and out all the time. I have a job. I eat out every night. I haven't shopped in weeks."

Tom shifted in his chair, but if he was surprised at his sister's tone and her lack of hospitality, he didn't show it. The girl started to say something, but Tom cut her off with a gesture of his hand.

"Hey, the last thing I want to do is put you out. Do whatever you have to do. We'll find something to eat. A couple of cans will do."

"I told you, I haven't shopped for ages." This last came out almost apologetically. Tom smiled.

"Ah, you've got yourself a steady, right?"

To her embarrassment and chagrin, Linda blushed. She could feel her cheeks flame up, her heart pound.

"I've made new friends, yes."

"One special friend, eh?"

"None of your business. Look, you never warn me you're coming, and this time," she plunged headlong into it, even as she regretted doing so, "you come with someone else. I just can't take care of two extra people for ten days!" There was a long silence. Bess coughed into a tiny fist. She had a round simple face but her eyes were dark and devious. Tom got up and stretched, still holding the glass.

"Well, I thought you might like to see me before such a long trip. God knows when I'll be back."

Linda shrugged in frustration. He might well be back before the end of the month, if past history meant anything. Tom never lasted long on any job. "That won't do, you know," she heard herself saying. She realized with sudden horror that she had dredged up the phrase from the dark well of her childhood, when Mrs. Ashton, her fourth grade teacher would stand in front of the room scolding one or another of her students. Her favorite phrase was "That won't do, you know," and she would scowl, her face dark and ugly. The look was enough for the girls; with the boys she would be more daring, taking hold of their shirt collars or sweaters and pushing them into the back of the room, facing the wall.

"You sound like an old schoolmarm," said Tom reading her mood with uncanny precision. Linda blushed again, this time in anger.

"Fine! Thank you. But it doesn't change anything. I can't have you staying here."

"We can't afford to go anywhere else." Of course. It always boiled down to money.

She turned and left the room, not trusting herself to answer. She could hear Bess whispering to Tom and her brother's snort by way of response. In the kitchen, she looked in the cupboard and found two small cans of salmon and a tomato in the refrigerator. The bread was stale but it would do if toasted. Surely the girl could manage for them. There was a half liter of coke in the fridge and the makings for coffee and tea.

Would that be enough? She went to her purse and took out a twenty-dollar bill. Clearly, they didn't intend to leave, but neither did Linda intend to stay home from work or skip meeting Victor just to come back and prepare dinner for them. It was worth the money not to come back to the apartment the next day.

One day at a time, she thought uneasily. Experience had forced her to face up to the unpleasant reality that, left alone in the house, Tom helped himself to whatever he wanted. Once she actually saw him taking money from her wallet. On another occasion, as he was trying to zip up his carry-all, she recognized a silver box her Aunt Rudie had given her for graduation. It was tucked under some shorts. She had never asked any questions, although he must have realized that she'd know things were missing. Well, she couldn't monitor his every move, but neither was she going to leave anything of value lying around this time!

Back in the living room, that first evening, she handed him the twenty-dollar bill and told him it would have to last them through the weekend. He raised his eyebrows in disbelief, but said nothing. In her room, she took her mother's two rings, her gold filigree brooch and silver earrings, and put them in her purse. Nothing for him to pick up and walk away with, as in the past. How had she tolerated all that? When she'd left in the morning, Tom and the girl were still asleep.

All through dinner, she was distracted, worried. Victor sensed her mood but asked no questions. They had gone to a small family restaurant a few blocks from the house, and later they walked to a nearby movie to see a Tom Hanks film. On the way home, she told him about her brother, the whole story, and how he had turned up again the night before, this time with a girl. He asked for no details. When she had finished, he commented: "Do what you think best. He's not a child." No indeed. He was no longer a moody teenager but a cunning man who had no scruples about stealing from his sister.

By the time she got in, they had gone to bed. The apartment was still and dark, except for the small night bulb in the corridor. She checked the kitchen. Everything seemed in place. They had obviously gone out to eat. Good. In her room she undressed and went to bed, uncertain how she would handle the situation the next day but too tired to think about it at that late hour. She had slept pretty soundly until the closing of the front door had forced her back to the present, to a murky dawn, and a question. Had they left? A glance into the spare room told her they were still there. The girl at least. It was Tom, then, she'd heard closing the front door. He must have gone out for something.

This morning she would leave earlier than usual. The twenty she'd given him two nights ago would have to carry them, even if he was, as he'd said, broke. Linda knew from experience that this was never quite the case. Tom always had some ready cash, enough for essentials if Linda didn't come through. No, this time she wouldn't give in.

He had not returned when she left for work at eight-fifteen, and the girl had not stirred. Linda propped a note against the sugar bowl. "Won't be back until late." She felt better, having made plans for the weekend coming up. After work on Friday, she and Victor would drive upstate, or go down into Pennsylvania. Victor would work out the details. She simply refused to stay in the apartment with Tom and the girl.

Returning home close to eleven that night, she was surprised to find Bess sitting by herself in the living room.

"I didn't expect you to be still up. Where's Tom?" She paused in the doorway, conscious of an aversion to stepping over the threshold and inviting conversation. Bess looked up at her.

"I don't know. He hasn't been here all day. Since last night."

Linda frowned. "You mean he never came back?"

"I didn't even know he had left."

"Well, I heard him close the front door early this morning, about seven." She found that she was inside the room, walking to the liquor cabinet. She poured herself some scotch. "Don't you know where he went?"

The girl shook her head. "We were supposed to check the plane reservations today." She shrugged. After a short pause, she went on. "Do you think he might have had an accident?"

"I doubt it."

"We should report him missing, maybe."

"But he's not missing, our Tom!" she replied with undisguised bitterness. "Just up to his old tricks. Look, he's got to come back for you and the luggage, right? So, not to worry." She didn't feel quite as sure as she sounded, but he couldn't disappear, not with the girl still there and his possessions all packed in those three bags. He probably wanted to make her sweat a bit for trying to get rid of them. Only, it wouldn't work. She wasn't going to cave in simply because he was acting like a child.

She said goodnight and went to bed. The next morning, she told the girl she wouldn't be coming back in the evening, she'd be gone all weekend. "You'll have to fend for yourself." The girl said nothing. "Oh, he'll turn up," she went on, as she held out some bills. The girl hesitated, then took the money. "I know it's not your fault, but I can't keep doing this, you know." Before leaving, she said: "I'll call tomorrow or Sunday, check on things, see if you're still here." She handed her a spare key to the front door. "You'll need it if he's not back yet and you want to go out for something to eat." She desperately hoped they'd be gone by the time she got back Sunday evening.

That evening, after a quick dinner, she and Victor drove into Pennsylvania and spent the night at a small inn he'd found listed on the Internet. On Saturday, they visited an Amish farm, bought some home made preserves to take back to the city, drove down into Delaware and checked into a motel just outside of Wilmington. The next day, Sunday, they'd gone to see the Fabergè exhibit and after lunch visited the pre-Raphaelite collection at the Delaware Art Museum. It was a glorious two days.

It started to drizzle as they came off the George Washington Bridge. By the time Victor left her outside the brownstone, the rain was coming down heavily. She realized, with a pang, that she had not once thought about Tom or the girl all the while she was with Victor.

"I'm back," she called out, as she switched on the light in the foyer. There was no answer.

She turned on other lights and went through the small apartment. The bags were gone, no sign of Tom or the girl. Linda drew a deep sigh of relief. Well, that was that! She loved her brother; but the man he had become and the distance that had grown between them, made even simple communication virtually impossible. She had a life of her own, nothing glamorous, just an ordinary life . . . and the very real possibility of an ordinary but pleasant marriage, eventually a family . . . .

She wondered if they had left anything to nibble on. Holding the refrigerator door open, she stood there and gaped at the stacked sealed paper trays of meat, assorted deli containers, fresh orange juice, milk, cream, large mangoes and persimmons, even a small container of fresh figs . . . . Was this a bad joke? She opened the kitchen cupboards. They too were full — cans of soup, beans, Dole pineapple juice, jams and jellies . . . . Frowning, she went into the living room and opened the liquor cabinet. Sure enough, there was a fresh unopened bottle of Dewars, as well as a bottle of Absolut, and Punt et Mes. Something churned inside her, waiting for release. A sliver of fear cut into her consciousness.

He had left the note inside her special drawer, where she kept the key to her safe deposit box, her bank book, passport, birth certificate, and her social security card. She picked up her bank book and flipped through it, almost carelessly, the knowledge of what had happened already a certainty in her mind. When she had opened the account, she had sent Tom a signature card to fill out, so that he could have access in case of an emergency. He was her brother, after all, the only family she had.

She stared at the balance of $2,000, the withdrawal of $18, 896.78 entered in the bank book on Friday. It seemed important to her just then to remember where she had been at the time, what she was doing that morning. She'd been sitting at her desk at work, of course, while her brother was stealing her life savings, adding irony to injury by filling her refrigerator and pantry with food and liquor. At five, she and Victor had gone to Fiore's for pasta, then driven off for the weekend. Had her brother left by then?

She didn't shy away from blaming herself, at the same time excusing her carelessness. Who would have dreamed he'd go this far? She'd always tried to give him what he needed; overlooked those times when he took what he wanted. She sat down on her bed, resignation settling over her, like a pall. She found it difficult to breathe.

After a while, still holding the bank book, she went back to the kitchen and shut the refrigerator door. In the living room, she poured herself some scotch and drank it slowly, standing by the liquor cabinet. She refilled the small glass and took it with her to the sofa. Not used to hard liquor, the scotch tasted harsh and medicinal, but soon she felt it taking effect. She sat very still for a long time, sipping her drink, the trauma of the discovery slowly giving way to a sense of urgency. Her mind cleared, her thoughts began to surface from where they had run for cover.

What would she tell Victor?

Although they had not spoken openly about it, an understanding existed between them. They had talked about purchasing a condo together. What would Victor say when he learned she couldn't afford it any more? An unfamiliar terror clutched at her. Would he — ? She could not begin to imagine life without Victor. The thought was unbearable. She could never go back to what she was before she met him. Without Victor, there was no life, she would cease to exist.

But Victor loved her . . . .

She forced her thoughts elsewhere. Even if she tracked her brother down — an effort in futility — the money, if there was any left, would be tucked away where she couldn't possibly reach it. In any case, Tom was an expert at covering his tracks. She would never be able to find him, unless or until he chose to surface. And no doubt he would, once he was settled in, wherever that was. She was certain it was not New Zealand.

And any legal action was out of the question. Both their names were on the bank records. Officially, Tom was entitled to draw on the account. He had remembered that. No, she had no recourse whatever.

She read the note. *Sorry, Sis. I'm really in a fix. This will help me get started again. No, not in New Zealand, but you guessed that, didn't you? I'll make it up to you, as soon as I can. Love, Tom (and Bess).*

Wide awake in bed later, she suddenly saw again the little Amish boy who had run after her as she and Victor were leaving the farm. The image flashed before her, the boy waiting for his father's nod of approval before handing Linda a sprig of fresh rosemary. The gesture had touched her in some inexplicable way. She had bent down to stroke his cheek. The boy had run away laughing. She remembered how soft his skin had felt.

Someday, she would have a son of her own . . . .

Tomorrow she would tell Victor. She shivered as though a cold hand had come to rest on her heart.

When she dropped off finally, it was a dark restless sleep. Light was beginning to filter through the blinds when she dreamt that Victor was standing in her doorway with a bouquet of roses. She smiled and invited him in.

"No, I can't stay," he said. "I have to run. Things will work out, you'll see." In the dream, she had stepped out on the landing and followed him to the stairs. As he started down, he looked at her, a small tense smile on his lips. She went back inside and took the flowers to the sink, where she arranged them in a large jar. There was a small card nestled among the pink and red roses. "You'll find someone else. Just be patient."

Awake, she felt drained. The apprehension she had felt in her dream seemed to have spilled into the overcast gray day.

At work, she was nervous, tense, unable to do more than shuffle papers on her desk. Early in the afternoon, she left, claiming she was coming down with something. She called Victor at work and he agreed to meet her earlier than usual at a small diner not far from the house.

She was already settled in a booth a good half hour before Victor came in, at five fifteen. He sat down next to her and kissed her lightly on the cheek.

"What's up?"

"Nothing really. I just wanted to see you. I've missed you. I always miss you when you're not with me." She touched his arm, trying to read his eyes. Nothing to read, she scolded herself. He doesn't know.

"I'm glad we were able to get away. It was fun, wasn't it?"

They ordered a light meal and a small carafe of wine. By the time they were finished, the place had begun to fill up. It was a popular place: the food was good, prices were reasonable.

Victor put his hand over hers. "What's wrong?"

She *had* to tell him. "My brother Tom showed up with this girl, last Tuesday . . . . "

"Yes, you told me."

"Sometime over the weekend, they took off again. I don't know where they've gone." Victor's look suggested curiosity, or was it a touch of irritation? "My brother," she added, "is unpredictable, unscrupulous." Victor frowned. She went on, miserable, hating herself for wanting to cry, not sure she could hold back the tears that threatened to gag her. "They were gone when I got home last night. I found a note. He'd been to the bank and . . . taken out most of my savings." She needed to watch as he took in what she had said. For a moment they stared at one another, then Victor lowered his eyes and began tracing a pattern on the plastic table surface. She went on almost breathlessly. "You see, after my father died and everything was settled, I opened up a new bank account, with Tom as a second signature. I never expected him to remember, much less do what he did." Her voice was unsteady. She felt the tears welling up behind her eyes. "I've always tried to help him. He didn't have to do that to me."

"That's terrible," said Victor, pulling himself up and settling back in his seat. "How much did he take?"

"Over $18,000. He left $2,000 in the account." Victor whistled softly. He shook his head. "That's awful."

"Of course, I make a good salary. And I don't spend much. I'll have it back in no time." Victor nodded. "People lose on the stock market every day, . . ." she concluded lamely.

"Well," he waved for the check, "but you're not people and you don't play the stock market."

Outside, he took her hand as they headed back toward Broadway. "It'll pass," he said. "You'll get over it."

"Yes, yes, of course."

At work, the next day she found a huge bouquet of assorted flowers. There was no note. She suspected Tom was trying to make up in his carefree way for having stolen her money.

After a hurried lunch in the cafeteria, she returned to her office and found several phone messages her assistant had taken down, including one from a Mr. Victor

Larsen. He couldn't meet her for dinner that evening, he had to be at an important briefing for an out-of-town presentation.

There was a message from him on her machine at home, also. Had she received the flowers? . . . . Sorry he had to be out of town for the rest of the week . . . . He'd call when he got back. "Things will work out," the message ended, "just be patient."

"Yes. Of course. I'll do that," she kept repeating as she got into bed, trembling, her face wet with tears.

SUMMER SOLSTICE

"Brad, you're not serious!"

"People outgrow one another. A person is stunted trying to keep up with the significant other. Be honest, don't you feel your interests, your own personal priorities have taken a new direction, that you've moved, okay okay, just a *little* bit away from Herb's? You still share things, sure, every couple living together does, but inside, where it counts, you're a different person from the Frances he married. Am I right?"

Frances Considine smiled, trying to hide the totally irrational embarrassment she experienced at having been singled out in that way and by someone she hardly knew. Brad Ingersoll, recently divorced, was spending a few days with their neighbors, Dick and Martha Orville, and had been invited with them to the Considine's cocktail party. "He's trying to find his bearings after a difficult divorce," Martha had told Frances.

She cast a veiled look at her husband, standing across the room by the patio door, engrossed in whatever it was that George Hartley was telling him. The Hartleys had bought an old mansion half a mile down the road, and, after dramatic renovations, had moved into it early in the spring. Herb had first met George on the 5:48 evening commuter train. George was in publishing. When he discovered Herb was a lawyer, he had picked his brain about author's rights and the wording of contracts. Herb didn't seem to mind. He found George good company on the ride home every evening. During the last seven weeks, Frances and Herb had taken their new neighbors to the club twice for cocktails and as their guests to the Memorial

Day dinner-dance. Their names had been put up for the Club by a number of old-timers, including Herb Considine. Herb had suggested the cocktail party to Fran ("a nice gesture"), since tonight the Hartleys would be formally recognized at the Club's annual dinner for new members.

George was connected in some distant way to the Roosevelts. He also had inherited lots of money. His wife's family originally came from Naples, but Gloria herself had grown up in New Jersey. Her father and grandfather were in real estate, with lots of political connections. "A de-hydrated Sophia Loren," Dick Orville had quipped, when he first spotted her at the Club. When asked what that meant he couldn't quite say, but yes there *was* a kind of resemblance in Gloria's wide smile, everyone agreed, her perfect teeth, her thick head of auburn hair, her slim waist and wide hips. Walter Tierney, chairman of the Club's membership committee, had offered: "What Dick is too shy to say" — "Ha, that'll be the day!" "Sure!!" "Dick *too shy to say?*" "Dick who?" rose a teasing chorus of friendly voices, while Dick smiled, thriving on the attention —"what he means is, Gloria is a very sexy lady!"

She was indeed. This particular evening, in Fran Considine's spacious high-ceilinged living room with its uncluttered French windows stretching across the whole length of the wall, overlooking the Hudson, Gloria Hartley sat on one of the white brocade sofas, a striking picture in a crimson georgette cocktail dress and a thin diamond and pearl choker around her Modigliani neck. She was a stunning portrait. Men found her irresistible but kept their distance. Even the women admired her. Perhaps it was her infectious down-to-earth laughter and her open display of affection for George that defused any potential jealousy. Even now, as she beckoned to her husband, who went to sit beside her on the sofa, she drew all eyes to her. Some of the women smiled as she stretched her smooth bare arm behind her husband's back and stroked his neck: it was a familiar gesture and the message was clear: Gloria did not pose a threat to any of them.

George reached back for his wife's hand, brought it around and kissed it. Gloria smiled a secret smile, without turning her head.

"Trouble with you, Brad," said Herb, walking over to where his wife was standing, "you want the rest of the world to share your misery." Brad had made no effort to hide his resentment at the huge settlement his former wife had managed to wrest from him.

"I bet if you had the guts to give me a straight answer, without any threat of repercussions, you'd agree with me that a man's entitled to one free and clear divorce in his lifetime. Like I said, we grow in different ways at a different rate. We're entitled."

"Who's we, Brad? What about us women?" Martha Orville interjected. "Aren't we entitled too?"

"Sure, but the whole business of alimony and support has got to go. Equality right down the line."

"That's hardly fair," said Gloria. "Women can't be expected to go into a new kind of lifestyle just because the husband decides to pick up his, what should we call it, his divorce option? Some wives may not be trained to fend for themselves."

"Maybe they should learn how — "

"What could I learn to do!" Gloria's hearty laugh filled the room. She half-turned where she sat to look at her husband, who leaned down smiling and whispered something in her ear.

Brad went on, somewhat peevishly: "Well, now, you're putting me on the spot, Gloria, and you know it. Right George?"

"You mean she's undermining the feminist cause? George asked by way of reply.

"More like, socially incorrect — " ventured Dick.

"I call it sexual harassment," said Martha Orville.

"Discrimination, is more like it," said Herb.

"I'm serious," said Brad. "Gloria is trying to be deliberately provocative."

"I'm not sure I understand," said George assuming a thoughtful frown.

"C'mon! Everybody knows an attractive woman can always fend for herself," said Brad with a bold grin, turning toward the array of liquor bottles on the long table set up between the open patio doors. He poured himself a large scotch and added a piece of ice.

"But why should she," offered Fran, glossing over the obvious connotations of Brad's remark. "Just because her husband decides *he's* ready for a divorce?"

"I see it in a different light," said Sylvia Grobanski, who was into her third marriage. Sylvia was the maverick among them. Sylvia spoke her mind, was always "frank" about expressing her views and always managed to insult someone or other as a result. Now she went on in her ringing voice: "Divorce is like any other commodity. Whoever wants it has to pay for it. If the husband initiates the divorce, whatever the reason, he's got to pay for it. If the wife wants to screw around on her own and wants to be free to do it, if she's got someone else waiting in the wings, well then, *she's* got to pay."

An embarrassed silence followed this statement. Sylvia's history was known to everyone for miles around. She was not a newcomer to the community or to divorce. She had been born somewhere in the midwest, in a Polish Jewish family of eight and had ended up on the Gold Coast before moving to Westchester with her current husband. Her first marriage to millionaire playboy Howard Dunlee Masters had made headlines but their divorce was an even more spectacular media event, a long drawn-out legal battle, which Sylvia had won. Her second marriage to a well-known international golf pro lasted fifteen months. That divorce was quiet by comparison since (rumor had it) Sylvia was willing to part with over a million to get rid of the guy and zoom in on her new target, Stanley Grobanski, CEO and Chairman of the Board of Littlejohn, Littlejohn and DeWitt, a world-wide pharmaceutical conglomerate. She and Stanley had been married for five years.

"What sort of payment would you suggest?" Brad asked, sipping his fresh drink.

"Forego all alimony? Give up the custody of the kids if there are any? Of course, if she's clever she'll get someone to wipe out her husband. But love is blind in more ways than one. We never seem to go for the obvious solution." She waved grandly. "Well, let's say, the most efficient one . . . . " The Orvilles stared at her. Fran turned away, and in so doing caught a strange secret smile on her husband's lips. George looked down at his wife's blood red nails. Gloria gazed up at some vital message on the ceiling.

Stanley got up from his chair and went to the bar for pretzels. Herb Considine joined him there.

"Well Stan, I'm glad you're still with us!" he said in a voice that was meant to carry across the room.

Sylvia tossed back her head and laughed. She was still an attractive woman at thirty-seven. Plastic surgery had helped her keep the years at bay, and all in all she had enough going for her to make people turn to stare. The women insisted she had had breast implants and that her hips had been reduced; but whatever alterations had been made, the result — even those who disliked her had to admit — was sensational. Her platinum blond hair couldn't possibly be natural (even if it had once been); but no one really knew, since her hairdresser remained a mystery. Even her maid (so the story went), bribed it was said by Helen Gorelick, the Club Commander's wife, could find no listing for a hairdresser in her employer's telephone book. Her skin had the peculiar translucency often seen in Nordic complexions, her eyes were the palest aquamarine. In a certain half-light, she might have been mistaken for an albino, except for the healthy color of her skin and the general impression of good solid genes. She used very little make-up, conscious of the startling effect she produced.

"Oh, don't worry about Stanley! Stanley is forever. Stanley is my rock, my rudder, my stud! Stanley and I have found our own common market at just the right time in life, isn't that so, sweetie?"

Stanley Grobanski turned where he stood at the bar and looked across the room at his wife. "Sylvia has written the book on the subject. Or someone has, under that same name and Sylvia has taken credit for it." His wife howled. Martha Orville looked confused. Her husband stared at the glass in his hand. Gloria cocked her head to one side and smiled at Sylvia.

George said: "Well, Sylvia, you can always count on me if you ever have to fend for yourself. I'll sign for your memoirs any time you're ready!"

"Ah, someone who's willing to take me on!" she replied, enjoying the moment. "But Brad's right, you know. Women ought to be able to fend for themselves."

"Work keeps idle thoughts at bay, both male and female." said Dick Orville to no one in particular, following some dirt track of his own.

"Well, well, well, where did you pick that up?" said Sylvia, making a face and peering at him as though he were some kind of specimen trapped under glass. "It almost sounds profound."

Orville blushed and cleared his throat. "The real question is," he went on, "how many suits, dresses, furs, whatever, can a person wear? How many cars do you need? And yet there's never enough. We're all gluttons about life and what we can buy in it. And when we've accumulated all the things we think we want, we look around for novelty, excitement with a new edge, at least the illusion of novelty when everything around us is jaded. That takes money, but is it really worth it? Sooner or later we all come to the same conclusion. In the end, all the designer items in the world aren't enough to satisfy us. Am I right ladies?"

"Oh, Dick, what a killjoy you are!" Sylvia replied. "Did you hear that, Stanley? You've wasted your best years making a fortune."

"No, darling," her husband answered. "Until you came along I wasted my best years looking for someone who could spend it with flair!"

"Now there's an intelligent man," was his wife's rejoinder. She'd gone up to him and now put her arm through his and went on. "Talk about flair! I'll always remember how Frank Sinatra used to charter a plane to pick up pizza from that place, in Trastevere was it, that he liked so much. 'The only pizza worth waiting for'," she mimicked. "The hitch is, how do you keep it really hot and fresh during the long flight back? Now, there's a real challenge for you, Dick," she continued lightly, turning to Orville, who was the head of an engineering firm. "How does one keep pizza fresh and really hot for six hours?"

"See?" Brad interjected before Dick could reply. "Some things money can't buy."

"Wrong again, dear man," said Sylvia. "You buy the place and bring it here with the chef, the special water, all the ingredients they claim make a difference. That way, you'll have your fresh pizza in the special brick oven you set up in your back yard, any time you want it. In the end, Frank was a cheapskate."

"Oh, I don't know about that," said Gloria. "He sure as hell threw money around when he wanted to."

"Did you know him well?" Martha Orville ventured.

"Frank? My grandfather knew his Mom. They were buddies from way back. I think they might even have been related in some way. A nephew twice removed was an usher at our wedding. Remember him George? What *was* his name! You almost signed him up to write a biography about Frank, but the deal fell through."

Brad laughed harshly. "Yeah, somebody probably threatened him!"

"Actually, Frank got wind of it, didn't like the idea, so the guy backed out," said George. His wife picked up a piece of stuffed celery from the dish on the table in front of the sofa and munched on it slowly.

All eyes turned to the doorway, as Dolores, the Considines' maid came in and whispered something to Fran. The two women left the room together, Dolores talking while Fran leaned slightly into her, listening. Herb watched his wife walk out and moved closer to where the others sat. He glanced at his watch.

When Fran reappeared, she motioned to her husband from the doorway. She seemed agitated. Herb listened intently as she whispered. He nodded, once or twice, then disappeared down the hall. Fran stood looking after him for a few moments, then came back inside the room.

George was having a mild argument with Dick over micro ovens and the dangers of radiation. Brad was talking animatedly with Stanley about media control of the news, while Martha listened. Gloria and Sylvia were carrying on about South American and French designers. When Fran reappeared, Gloria waved for her to join them and Fran went to sit down between the two women.

"Something wrong?"

"Sam, Herb's son, is on the phone. He lives with his mom in Beverly Hills."

"Do they call often?"

"What? No. In fact, *she* never calls." She fell silent for a moment, frowned, went on: "Herb doesn't want to talk to her, it's always a quarrel. At one point, he told her to have Sam call and relay her messages, whatever she had to say." A trace of irritation had crept into her voice. She went on quickly, almost to herself, her eyes fixed on the corridor: "The boy was terribly upset about something."

Both women glanced up as Herb came back into the room, looking grim. Fran got up and went to him. "What's wrong, honey?"

A hush fell over the assembled group. Outside, the light had turned into a picture-postcard chaos of color. The river had taken on a silver sheen with bands of violet and rose and red where the swollen sun spread its dying fire across the water. A slight breeze had come up, but the air was still hot from the day's unrelenting, unseasonably high temperature.

Herb put his arm around his wife but spoke to the entire room. "I'm sorry. I have some bad news. That was Sam, my son. He called to tell me my ex-wife Jean was found dead just about an hour ago. She drowned in the pool behind the house." There were gasps, murmurings, startled looks. Fran tried to read her husband's face. She heard herself asking:

"How could that have happened? You told me she couldn't swim, never went into the pool."

"I don't know."

Herb stared down at his glass. Now he finished the contents in one gulp and walked over to the bar, where he poured himself some neat gin and drank it down before turning back to his guests. They were all watching him.

"I'm sorry. That's all I know," he said in a tight voice. "I'll have to fly out there as soon as I can."

Fran turned to her guests. "I'm terribly sorry." The Grobanskis were the first to move out. Sylvia kissed Fran

lightly on the cheek and whispered to her. Brad patted
Herb's arm and said something to Fran, before joining the
Orvilles as they left.

George Hartley walked over to where Fran was
standing.

"What can we do, Fran? Tell me. We want to help."
She nodded, her eyes riveted on Gloria who was standing
next to Herb, her hand placed lightly on his arm. She was
whispering with an intensity that Fran could only associate
with a very special kind of intimacy. There was something
private, ominous, about the way they stood, trying not to
get too close, the hurried exchange of words. George went
on: "If Herb has to be away into next week, come join us
on the yacht. No point staying alone in the house. Herb
can reach you on the boat, if he has to." She nodded again,
the drone of his voice barely registering.

It was only a matter of seconds. Then Herb caught
his wife staring and said something to Gloria, who quickly
turned and hurried over to join her husband.

"Fran, dear, I'm so sorry. I was just suggesting to
Herb, why don't you come stay with us while he's away?"

"I told her the same thing," said George.

Fran did not answer. Herb had freshened his drink
and now joined them. He put his arm around Fran's waist.
His eyes darted to her face, scanned it surreptitiously when
she moved slightly away from him. Gloria asked: "How
long will you be gone?"

"I'm not sure. A few days. Maybe a week. It all
depends."

"Well, Fran, you're more than welcome to stay with
us as long as it takes," Gloria went on. Her look was direct,
unrevealing. Fran did not answer. Her gaze rested on the
thin shadows beginning to spread over the sun-drenched
tiles of the patio. George looked down at his shoes. Herb
frowned, his eyes darting around the room as he sipped his

drink. It was almost nine. The longest day of the year. Gloria broke the uncomfortable silence. "Of course, it's not as though she was really part of the family — "

George scowled at his shoes. "Family enough. It's Herb's son out there."

Gloria said soothingly. "Darling, all I meant was, the woman has been out of Herb's life for years now. What is it, ten? Twelve?" She glanced at Fran, but Herb answered.

"We were divorced seven years ago. Sam was nine."

"Poor kid!" said George, with genuine concern. "Isn't there anyone else out there for him?"

"No. Well, Jean has a cousin in San Diego. But, they've never been close."

Fran seemed to come out of her reverie. "Better call the airlines if you want to catch a plane tonight." She bent down to pick up some crumbs from the sofa and placed them on the large tray Dolores had brought in to clear away glasses and dishes.

Gloria and George moved toward the door.

Fran said something to Dolores, who nodded and went upstairs. Herb had sat down on the sofa, his elbows resting on his knees, his head in his hands, staring down at the carpet.

The Hartleys hugged Fran and left. She could hear their car moving slowly down the long driveway, the crunch of tires on the roadway pebbles filling the silence of the room.

"Do you want me to make the call?"

Herb looked up. "No, I'll do it."

"I told Dolores to take out two bags."

Her husband gave her a searching look from where he sat. "Is something wrong?" He rose and walked toward her. Fran moved forward to the patio entrance and stood looking out over the water. The sun had disappeared below the horizon.

"She's dead. Isn't that something wrong?"

"I mean, you're acting strange."

"Am I?"

"Have I said something — ?"

She turned back into the room and started to place glasses and dishes on the large tray Dolores had brought in earlier. An incomprehensible fear took hold of her. A few seconds had changed her life. She could not ignore that simple fact, even if she could not explain it.

Oh, there was something there between them, of that she was sure. But what exactly? No doubt they were lovers, but that hurried whispering, the sense of urgency suggested something more. Or were her instincts playing tricks on her? Could Jean possibly have been . . . ? No, no, she wouldn't entertain, even for a minute, such a macabre thought. Of course, it was a joke among them, Gloria's connections; but, no, it couldn't be anything like that! Jean had made outrageous demands, but Herb had always been able to deal with them. She'd never been a threat!

Yet, even as she tried to unravel her intuitive grasp of some dreadful reality, she knew there was more than fantasy behind her fear. Herb had adjusted to the divorce, the alimony, Jean's recurring demands for extra money. When exactly had she begun to notice a change? For there *had* been a change. A harsher tone in Herb's voice when he gave Sam messages for his mother, a warning, once, that he would have his lawyers examine her tax returns, have her watched, even . . . . It had all started a few months ago, ever since —

He had come up behind her. She could smell the gin on his breath. Quickly she moved away, straightened up the sofa and chairs.

"Do you expect to be gone the whole week?"

"At least. I have to bury her, you know. Among other things." She ignored the sarcasm in his voice.

"I'll help Dolores pack." She moved quickly out into the hall and almost ran up the stairs, breathless. Dolores was sorting out shorts and socks.

What was it he had said just the other morning? If only Jean would marry again, get out of his life. At the time she had commiserated with him. Jean had just had Sam call to ask for several thousand dollars to cover extra expenses as Sam entered his senior year in high school. Herb loved his son, but he knew that only a small part of what he sent Jean for Sam's "extra expenses" were spent on the boy. Until recently, he had sent the money without too much fuss, although ample provision had been made for Sam in the divorce settlement, which also had won Jean a huge cash sum, in addition to much else. Was it guilt that had never made her question the extravagant cost of that divorce? Now, suddenly, that extravagance bothered her as it never had at the beginning, when she was so much in love with him and nothing else really mattered. At the time she had felt giddy with happiness, that he would sacrifice so much for her, for plain unadulterated Fran.

She was twenty-seven, Herb thirty-eight, when they married soon after his divorce became final. She'd met him when her first book had been accepted by Dutton and a friend suggested she show the contract to a good lawyer before signing it. Herb had come highly recommended.

Well, Jean was out of the picture now. Jean had drowned in her pool in the Beverly Hills mansion Herb had bought for her as part of their settlement. And Sam would not be a teenager forever. Sam would soon be off to college, would marry, would be earning his own living.

But she, Fran, would still be around. How much would he be willing to pay to get rid of *her*?

Surely she was indulging in grim fantasies! Herb loved her. They'd not had a serious quarrel all the time they'd been married . . . .

Gloria's laughing face flashed before her. She heard again the throaty voice, saw the slim hand resting on Herb's sleeve, the intense whispering, the unmistakable bond revealed in those few shattering seconds when they seemed to forget where they were. The look on Herb's face as he caught his wife staring at them across the room made her tremble. She sat down on the edge of the bed. She saw again his quick adjustment, saw Gloria's hand withdraw as he said something to her, recalled her look as she hurried back to where Fran and George were standing —

It had been only a matter of seconds, their two heads close, almost touching. She tried to brush the memory aside by picking up the jacket she had laid down on the bed.

"He'll want this blazer, Dolores, but make sure we send it to the cleaner's when he gets back." Dolores took the jacket, folded it and placed it in one of the bags. Herb had come into the room.

"There's a flight at eleven-fifty from Kennedy. I've called the limo. Are we almost packed?"

She nodded. Dolores left the room. Herb glanced at the items neatly arranged on the top of the two open bags. "You'll be all right?"

"Of course."

"I'll call as soon as I get there."

At the door, with the limo waiting, he turned back to her. "Would you mind if I took Sam home with me? We'll have to put him up for a while. Maybe until school starts again."

"Of course. Why should I mind?"

He kissed her on the cheek and was gone. She watched the limo turn at the gate and disappear into the thick trees that lined the private access road to the house. She stood there staring at the empty road for a few more seconds, then went back inside.

Alone now, she was surprisingly calm. No, it was wrong of her to entertain the suspicions that had crowded into her mind, her heart. She was overwrought by the news about Jean.

With a start, she realized her fist was still closed over the crumpled slip of paper she had found in the blazer pocket. She couldn't remember crushing it into this small pebble. Carefully, she smoothed it over.

There was a phone number in Queens checked off, together with a name she recognized from the heavy media coverage it had elicited all through a spectacular trial which had ended with a predictable sentencing, all through the first few weeks when the convicted man was adjusting to a life sentence behind bars. She stared at the date and time, the brief message underneath the name, and at the bottom of the slip, the initial "G."

In the spreading dusk, she saw again her husband's face as he caught her staring at them across the room. For that brief moment, without warning, their eyes had locked in surprise and discovery. Then, as if a curtain had fallen between them, he had looked away. She wondered how feelings could change in an instant but knew with absolute certainty that in that moment her husband had become a stranger, someone she didn't know, perhaps had never really known, a stranger to whom she was nonetheless bound. In a flash of recognition she saw that the stranger her husband had become was also the enemy into whose hands she had fallen.

She tried to picture his expression when, alone, later, he would find the slip of paper missing from his blazer pocket.

SOHO REVISITED

Standing on the familiar street, the years between had dissolved under his prurient excitement. Soho. Earl's Court. The tube station. The newstand where once again he, Steve Horst, leafed through the porno magazines. The same notices taped on the wall outside the tube station, the same subtle sensation threatening to wash over him and drown his new Spring of good intentions.

Dominatrix . . . . Male model . . . .Young girl: noon to 11 PM . . . . Rubber and leather for sale . . . .

Freddy had called it morbid lust. What did Freddy know, forgodssake!

The girl had not touched him but he felt her close by . . . . Well, yes, morbid lust was part of it. The thrill of obscenity, the pull toward unbearable pleasure, at once inviting and repelling.

Try it, you'll like it!

Freddy had once described the night time of the world as puppets in a beehive of creaking beds. "Go on, do it!" he'd said. "Looking on and drooling won't cure you. "

Neither had doing it. Maybe it was a residue of the Seminary and Father Casey's repeated references to St. Augustine, his constant reminder that not all actions are justified for the sake of experience. He'd read to them from the *Confessions:* "What is peace? The rapist finds his peace in attacking women. The murderer finds his peace in killing. The thief — "

The girl nudged him with her full breasts. Steve could see the nipples hard and big under the thin jersey.

Maybe he should have gone on to become a priest, after all. With Freddy once, savoring the obscenities along

Forty-Second Street, the porno and movie ads, the walking temptations, Freddy had blurted out: "You think you're virtuous because you look and don't taste? That's not virtue, Steve! Virtue is not even being aware of the temptation any more! Ask any alcoholic if that isn't the ideal cure. It may not happen, but that's what it should be! And you don't have it, kiddo. You're still fooling yourself that you can resist. Well, I say you can't. Not if you persist like this. It's like scratching a scab. It'll never go away as long as you keep scratching."

Maybe Freddy was right. Maybe he was still a priest at heart.

But sex had driven him from his large ambition, his long dream. And when he finally indulged, let himself go, he gave up everything else as hypocritical. That ocean of need washing over his best intentions, dragging them down as each wave receded, leaving him satiated yet restless all over again, each wave cresting into the next — how could he hold back something so powerful?

As usual, he had waited too long, opportunity had strolled away. He saw the girl moving slowly down the street toward a man who had been eyeing her. They spoke briefly then walked off together.

Ah, and there was the pub! Did he really expect to see again those people with whom he had drunk himself into oblivion so often the last time around? Dave, the carpenter who worked only to drink and who had a wife and a boy in Smyrna, Delaware of all places. Once, Steve had ventured: "Why don't you get a divorce?" "She's a bloody Catholic," Dave had answered with a grimace. And Ivan Stepnovanic, the transplanted cab driver from Macedonia, who had stayed with his sister and brother-in-law until they found him a girl from Skopje to marry and now was a British subject. Ivan was a great story teller. Even blind drunk, he was entertaining.

They weren't exactly friends, nor were they the kind of clientele you saw in singles bars. Here there were no preliminaries, no excuses, nothing but hard drinking, cursing, and whatever else followed naturally. A bunch of cave men, sodden drunk by the dawn's early light. Steve had often wondered how they were able to drag themselves to work the next day. Watching them night after night, he'd concluded that they found no real pleasure in their drinking. They would have been surprised to hear him say that, even more shocked to learn that Steve interpreted their nightly oblivion as a scarred effort toward happiness. He saw them as fellow travelers in Limbo, destined for much worse, belligerently claiming independence in the midst of their addiction to self-indulgence. He should know; he was a self-righteous bastard himself . . . .

He glanced at his watch. Five-ten. Inside he ordered a beer. Sipping, he glanced around. Early for the usual crowd, but already there were half a dozen men at the bar; by nine or ten o-clock the area where he stood would be four deep with hardly any elbow room to reach out for a fresh drink. Some of the small tables along the wall were already occupied.

He scanned the faces around him. The younger crowd had not yet taken over, thank God! Most of the men at the bar were about Steve's age. The place still had the threatening atmosphere he remembered. Not a place for tourists . . . .

Helen had fit right in. God, they had been good together! The best thing that had ever happened to him was Helen and her twisted ankle. They had met in July, when he had gone into a tiny card and novelty shop near the British Museum. She had limped from behind the counter to look for a map he wanted of the tube stations. It was late in the afternoon, he had been working in the Museum library most of the day and was ready for his usual evening routine. She was getting ready to go home. Impulsively he had asked if he could give her a lift. Then, in the cab, he had asked her to accompany him to the pub.

It become their home base, their special hangout, when they weren't in bed. What had happened to those two people? That last night just before he flew back to the States, back to his teaching after a nine-month sabbatical leave, she had been confused, disturbed. She had never made any demands on him, and she didn't on that last night, although he was ready to entertain them. It had started with a grim kind of exchange. She had said, while they lay in bed, smoking, in between sex:

"Intellectuals are notoriously poor fuckers."

"Mary Astor said the best lover she ever had was S. J. Perelman."

"Who the hell is S. J. Perelman."

"He was an intellectual.

"Don't try to get out of it," she'd answered, getting up and refilling their glasses with the cheap Australian wine Steve had bought. "Anyway, Perelman was a Jew."

"I thought you didn't know him — "

"Fuck the subtleties . . . ."

"How do you fuck the subtleties, show me." She usually would rise to the bait and give back in kind, but on this occasion she just kept rattling on.

"Gimme gimme gimme, you're a taker, grabbing at everything." She had turned angry eyes on him, standing by the bed looking down at him as he lay naked on the damp sheets they had shared. He had suddenly felt humiliated, somehow guilty. He had sat up on the side of the bed, his back to her, and rubbed his hair, waiting for her mood to dissipate. Instead she came around the bed to face him head on. "For you, it's like a disease." She had grown irritable, resentful. "Even with Greta Garbo!" She moved away with a disgusted toss of her thick auburn hair.

"What's Greta Garbo got to do with it?"

"I don't forget anything, you know. Not a damn thing. You're running after her still, you're infatuated with her, you'll never get over it, you told me once that only Greta Garbo could give you — "

"Shit! What's got into you!!" He jumped up angrily and moved past her toward the galley kitchen. He poured himself a large glass of water and drank it down almost in a single gulp. "You stupid bitch!" he heard himself yelling as he returned to the bedroom, carrying a second glass of water. "If you're starting your fucking period just get the hell out of here until it's over. I don't need this kind of aggravation."

She was quiet then. After a while, she sat down across the room and watched him as he put down the glass and lay down again, his arms locked behind his head, and stared at the cracked ceiling. When she spoke, it was as though all the madness had been drained out of her.

"I've been thinking of going back to the States. Oh, nothing to do with you, but I'm ready to tackle it I think. Here is, well it's like Purgatory, neither good nor bad, just something that can't survive. It's got to get better or worse . . . . But I'm not quite ready for hell . . . ." He didn't answer but she knew he was listening. "I may even have a job waiting, if I want it. My sister got married last month, she's living in Fort Lee. That's in New Jersey. She can put me up for a while, says there's always some kind of work to be had, if I'm not too choosy." He grunted, and she went on: "You don't think I could settle down in a place like that? Anyway, I'm coming close to trying."

He raised his head to look at her. It had to be now.

"I don't have to tell you how I feel." He held up his hand as though warding off any objections. "Just listen to me. I listened to you, right? . . . . There's no reason we can't try it together. I've wanted to say it, to ask you, but I wasn't sure how you felt, how you'd react. So, now I'm asking. Why don't we go back to the States together?"

She got up and paced restlessly across the tiny bedroom, waving her hands and spilling some of the wine in the process.

"No, no. Nothing like that. Fort Lee I can handle, maybe. My sister I can handle. But you, you're very strange. I can't trust myself to stay with you indefinitely." She stopped at the foot of the bed then, a long tortured look distorting her features. She seemed suddenly old and ugly. Steve got up and went to put his arms around her. She didn't resist.

"I'll give you plenty of space, all the time you want." When she didn't answer, he tilted her face so that she was forced to meet his eyes. "Can't we work it out? I want to, Helen. I really want to."

"I know," she said pulling away resolutely. Steve felt his heart sink. Her tone told him she had already reached a decision and that he wouldn't like it.

"Can we leave it open? I have to go back, classes begin on — "

"It was just an idea I had," she interjected, with an impatient wave, "but I don't think it'll work."

When she left, a short time later, Steve knew he wouldn't see her again . . . .

"Hey, old buddy! Is it really you!!" Steve jumped out of his reverie to see a large bearded man standing beside him, peering into his face."

"Dave! Dave Spingarn, you old sot! I was just thinking about you!"

"Hell no, you never had that expression on your face for *me*! Are you back to stay?

"Just for the summer. I'm doing a new book."

Dave rolled his eyes to the ceiling in mock horror. "How many people read your last one? Jackie Collins, now, she keeps us poor slobs drooling and gets millions for it. How much did you take in on your last book? Is this another one about the War of the Roses, all that crap?"

"Hey, forget my books! I'm here. Back where the action is."

"Yeah, well, things have changed a bit."

"*You* haven't —

"Matter of fact, I have. I mean, I'm not alone any more." And when Steve snickered and looked at him expectantly, his head cocked to one side, Dave laughed: "Nah, nothing like that. My wife I'm talking about. She decided to come over with the kid, after all. Hey, I'm not getting any younger. And, well . . . . We manage."

Steve settled into the kind of expression Dave was obviously trying to search out in the other's face. "Hey, I know all about it. Remember Helen? I tried to get her to go back with me. No dice. But, who knows? I'm not giving up!" Dave seemed surprised, caught off guard. "You *do* remember Helen, don't you?" Dave studied his beer.

"Sure, sure. Dark red hair. Good looking."

"Have you seen her around?" He tried to sound casual. Dave shrugged non-committedly.

"Not really. Maybe Gordon knows." He nodded at the tall balding man behind the bar.

"Yeah. Well, it's not important. I was just curious."

"Four years is a long time . . . . But, . . . look at *you*. Never thought I'd see you again!"

"Yeah. Zoomed right in on automatic pilot." They both laughed. Dave said:

"I work the first shift in a security outfit now, eight to four. Big office building, benefits, the works. I come in here to unwind before going home."

"No time for binges anymore . . . ."

"What the hell, there's more to life than getting stinking drunk."

"Right." There was an uncomfortable pause. After the first exuberant flush of recognition, conversation lagged. After two more beers, Dave had turned heavy and mopey. Steve hoped he would finish his drink and head for home. Instead he put down his empty glass and said:

"I guess you'll find out sooner or later so I might as well tell you, just in case you really came to check her out. Helen's around and kicking all right. She's gone into S and M. Right here in the area. You're bound to run into her sooner or later. I'm sorry Steve."

He felt the bile rising into his mouth. "What for? I don't own her. Never did."

"Well, I thought for a while back there you had something going."

Steve held up his glass, pointed to both of them for refills. When the drinks came, he said: "To the present."

Dave said: "To us."

"To you and the new life."

"To a great book."

"Yeah. My first best-seller."

They drank some more. To Steve it was as if a heavy gate had slammed down, jolting them into another reality. After a while, Dave waved to someone at the end of the bar and, excusing himself, moved away . . . .

Much later, through the smoke-filled noisy room, he saw Dave lean unsteadily over a woman at one of the tables, guffaw at something she said. So he was still here, and wifey was still waiting for him at home. Or was that just another one of his jokes? For a moment he felt as though he should follow up on it. It seemed important, just then, to verify whether or not Dave's wife was waiting for him at home. Steve burped. When had he changed to malt scotches? He remembered he hadn't eaten anything but a sandwich around noon. He asked the barman for an American hamburger and when told they had hamburgers but they weren't American, he hurled his drink against the mirrored wall behind the bar, breaking a bottle of gin and his own glass. The mirror remained intact.

Dave elbowed his way over to where the barman had called him:

"Look at that, will you? Get your bastard friend out of here pronto, before I mop the floor with him and then have him locked up!"

"Hey, don't blame me! I haven't seen this guy in four years!" Dave pulled Steve away from the bar. Gordon counted the change lying there and put it in his pocket.

"I'll absorb the rest. Just get him the hell out!"

On the sidewalk, Steve seemed to have difficulty orienting himself. "That was dumb!" said Dave.

"What, what, what — "

"You stupid jerk!'

"Yerwifswaiting — "

"Yeah, she'll wait. Can you make it home?" Dave was obviously in a hurry to be rid of him.

Steve nodded. He felt miserable.

Alone, he waited for his head to stop spinning. Soho was pulsing with activity now. It was after midnight. He stumbled over to the tube entrance. They were all there, an assortment of all sizes shapes and colors. Nausea gripped him and he doubled over. After he had vomited, he scanned again the faces around him. One of the girls started toward him, but her friend pulled her back and whispered something. They turned away laughing.

His body ached. He focused his mind on the need to get back to his rooming house. He walked a few steps then stopped as a huge black man came striding down the street, a small blond in shorts trying to keep up with him. They seemed purposeful and detached. Steve followed them with his eyes until they disappeared down one of the side streets. They had triggered something in his memory, a similar couple he had seen the last time he was in Soho. They too had walked past him, just like the couple he had just seen; days later he had watched them on a huge movie screen, twisting and pulling and moaning in the studied lust of experts acting out the fantasies of others.

A girl stepped out of a doorway down the street. He wanted to call out but his lips were parched and his throat raw. She was wearing white leather boots and a dark poncho over a striped mini-skirt. Under the streetlight her thick long hair glowed like buried embers. She watched as he started toward her, as he stumbled and fell to the curb. When he looked again, she was gone.

Later, much later, awake in an unfamiliar room, he stared down at the girl beside him. Her large mouth was loose in fitful sleep, her thin body darkly naked on the bare mattress. In sudden exasperation, he reached out and gripped her breasts until she let out a small scream and opened her eyes. He pulled her off the bed and forced her to the floor, on her knees. Outside he could hear the steady patter of rain. Afterward, he went to the grimy window and looked for some familiar landmark. Where was he? It was very dark outside. He couldn't make out anything. Even the street seemed to have disappeared.

The soft click of the door closing brought him back into the room. The girl was gone. He put on his clothing, picking up each piece slowly from the floor, where he had obviously thrown it earlier. It had turned cold, the rain was coming down hard now. Luckily, he had not ventured too far from the tube. He could walk home all right. He started off purposefully, his head down. Two drunks were sitting on the curb in the rain, resting against each other. The pub was closed.

It was still dark, the morning would be overcast at best. His watch told him it was just past five. Across the way he saw the door from which the girl in the white boots had emerged, earlier. He went up to it and stared at the brass knocker. From the abyss within him, the opening lines of a familiar poem surfaced unexpectedly:

> *Lo! Thus, as prostrate, in the dust*
> *I write my heart's deep languor and my soul's*
> *sad tears* . . . .

Another city. Another night. Another century. Closer than this present one, even though he shared this same rain, the same sun with her, would share this corner of time with her to the very end, she who was infinitely closer and yet more distant than anything in his city of dreadful night, where a lifetime ago he had staked out his godless heaven, his self-inflicted hell.

"IF I SHOULD WAKE . . . ."

Listening to his wife's breathing as she lay next to him — sol *do* sol *do* sol *dooooo* — an irritating musical refrain intruding on his cocoon-close sleepless night, Benny could not help comparing the sound with Hattie's voice when awake. It was as though she willed to remain *on,* like a night light. Her breath, as she slept, had the erratic pulse of her mindless accusations, the cajoling rhythm of her familiar complaints.

In the evening, at the dinner table, with her captive audience of one, she was especially versatile as she wove in and out of her husband's threadbare resistance with her awesome single-mindedness. Indefatigable in her claim for attention, she usually got what she wanted: — a new light fixture or approval of her middle east policy. When her mother "had had it" and moved to a studio apartment in Florida — one of the few times Hattie didn't get her way — she had told her daughter: "Hattie, you're spinning your wheels and don't know it."

The children had gone their separate ways, too. Sara was in California, married, with two children, and had just started her own small real estate agency. Her husband Rod, a quiet man, had not seemed to mind Hattie during the four months he and Sara stayed with her parents, right after they were married and Rod was looking for a new job. He had several offers but chose to go with a computer firm near Los Angeles, to Hattie's dismay. It was clear that even undemanding Sara had realized the pressing need to get as far away as soon as possible. Nothing Hattie said could change their minds. "Why way out there, for heavenssake! There are plenty of good computer outfits right here, or in

Connecticut!" Hattie had argued. Before they left, Sara had sought out her father and apologized to Benny, as though she was abandoning him. They had glossed over the obvious. Benny didn't want his daughter to feel any guilt. She deserved better than she'd had growing up, when Hattie's strident assertiveness threatened to break down the girl's fragile self-confidence.

His older daughter, Leslie, was strong-willed, but even as an obstinate teenager she knew when to back off and give in to her mother. At times, Benny was convinced that Leslie put forward certain requests just so she could appear to relinquish them and earn points with Hattie for being "sensible." At first, her goal had been *big money.* Hattie had no trouble interpreting her daughter's ambition as the acquisition of a rich husband. She was all for it. Benny, on the other hand, found his daughter's attitude crude and distasteful. But Leslie's priorities changed dramatically when Roy Anderson came into her life. She admitted that what she thought she wanted didn't always turn out to be the best thing — two husbands, both very successful, with lots of money, had proved the point. With Roy, she had discovered, to everyone's surprise, including her own, very different goals and a potential for hard work. Soon after their marriage, she and Roy had started a mail order company specializing in household gadgets. It had gone well; they were now looking into TV possibilities, like the Home Shopping Center. With Roy, Leslie was a new person — just as smart as before, just as practical and determined, still *driven,* but in a totally new direction. The new business tapped a rich vein of creativity in her, which Roy's experience as an engineer helped to mine. They worked well and were happy together. To Hattie it was riches to rags, are you kidding? An engineer?

As usual, when he thought about his three children, Benny left Kenneth for last. It was hard to think about his son without experiencing deep but often contradictory emotions. He hated Hattie's constant complaining about Kenneth, but he had to admit that there was a core of truth in them. The boy (boy? he was thirty-five!) had been a problem from way back. Not in the usual sense, not drugs or anything like that, but as far back as Benny could remember, Kenneth had never been able to cope easily, at best his timing was off. Or, if he did pick up something with energetic determination, he often backtracked and was unable to carry it through. Except for his painting.

He had majored in fine art at Boston University, where he had turned down a scholarship for graduate work to return to New York and paint. That had been thirteen years ago. It was the only thing he wanted to do (he had tried to explain to his father).

Lately, however, Benny found himself wondering if his son had begun to have some doubts about his talent. He seemed to have recognized an impasse. A tenacious purpose seemed to have replaced the early exuberance. Aside from the obvious difficulties of breaking through in the art world, where contacts were so immensely important (even Benny, who was not an art connoisseur, knew that), other realities had begun to surface. Kenneth's efforts to achieve a suggestive realism that bordered on the abstract suggested instead unfinished canvases. In the local library Benny had read up on Van Gogh, Klee, Rockwell, Picasso. In all of them he recognized clear vision, firm strokes, unambiguous form, a provocative combination of line and color, which seemed to have been effected effortlessly in every case. By comparison, his son's work showed an uneven skill and lacked cohesion. On his rare visits to the Village studio/loft Kenneth shared with his roommate from college, Johnnie Stillman, Benny would cast surreptitious looks at the unfinished canvases resting on easels and against the walls. He would come away with the troubling thought that Kenneth had been left behind. The one time he had struck out in a different direction — an attempt at cubism — he had aroused a flurry of interest on the part of a well-known art dealer. Johnnie had whispered to Benny about it (while Kenneth was preparing coffee in the curtained area that served as kitchen), eliciting from him the promise that he would not let on he knew. Nothing came of it. He found out later that the dealer had asked for more of the same, but Kenneth would not oblige. To Benny, it was all very confusing. He respected his son's decisions but could not understand them.

Hattie's oppressive concern discouraged Kenneth from visiting his parents on a regular basis. Benny had tried to make his wife understand that their son needed encouragement not criticism.

"That's not a life," was her constant refrain.

"So, what's a life?" Benny would ask.

"A regular job somewhere."

"What kind of job? Kenneth is not Rod, he's not Roy or anyone else for that matter. Why don't you just leave him alone."

"He's not getting anywhere, that's why. He's thirty-five and still where he was thirteen years ago. If you weren't blind to his faults, you'd know I'm right."

"Hattie, it's enough that *you* know you're right. The rest of the world can be spared!" he had said angrily and walked out of the house.

At the time he left home for college, Kenneth had admitted to his father that he had chosen Boston to get away from his mother's nagging. It was early in July, the summer was still ahead of them, when Kenneth announced that he was leaving for Boston to "settle in early and look around." Back in New York, he visited his parents once or twice a month, at first, then even less frequently, as time went by. For Benny, it was a wrenching; but soon, father and son worked out an arrangement so that they could meet for lunch once or twice a month. It served. By tacit agreement, Hattie was never told about those meetings. She would never have been able to grasp (or forgive) Kenneth's visiting with his father that way, without Hattie around. But only without Hattie around were father and son able to talk easily, freely, without tension.

On one of those occasions, Benny had asked: "Why don't you give Mr. Halstein more paintings like the ones he sold for you last year?" Abe Halstein owned a gallery in mid-town Manhattan and had exhibited some of Kenneth's semi-abstract canvases. "If there's a market for them — " But Kenneth had interrupted:

"What I gave Halstein were just experiments, Dad. I really don't care for that kind of painting, I don't feel comfortable with it. And I'm not going to waste my time just to please him. I've got some good paintings, if he wants them. The truth is, he's in there for a quick profit. He told me so, himself." Benny had remained silent and Kenneth had continued, as though convincing his father was important to him. "I can't spend valuable time trying to give him or anyone else what he thinks will sell. I'd rather starve."

Well, he *was* practically starving.

Kenneth seemed to have taken it all in stride. If, somewhere along the line, he had come to measure the limits of his talent and was disappointed in what he found, he gave no clue.

Still, Kenneth's call to his parents the night before had left Benny with an uneasy feeling. His son told them about a new exhibit that was almost ready, about plans for the summer at an art colony in Maine, possibly a part-time consultant's job in a gallery later in the year ("whatever that means, it's got to be better than selling brushes!"). In answer to Hattie's invitation to stop in for supper he said there was a lot to do, he was tired, he was looking forward to a few days' rest with friends, out on the Island, but he'd stop by briefly to see them on the way there. Hattie couldn't understand why he didn't come home to rest. "What's so special about the Island? Just getting there is the pits!" Kenneth, as usual, let his mother talk, then went on to something else.

It was while brooding about his son's call, hearing the echo of some unspoken disappointment in Kenneth's subdued voice, which also gave off unmistakable signs of weariness, that Benny came to a decision. It was not a sudden one, by any means; he had fantasized for over a year about going off with Crissy and starting a new life. But he had delayed, knowing that, once he was gone, his son Kenneth would be an easy target for Hattie's anger and resentment.

Benny had reviewed the entire plan carefully. It would work, he knew. Kenneth's call convinced him that the time had come to put the plan into motion.

Crissy was an important part of his decision. At first, she had simply been a pleasant encounter, but that turned very soon into a powerful attraction, then an affair. She was divorced, much younger than Benny, a high-salaried computer analyst working in the same building (they had met last Christmas, at an office party, where several companies had merged for the occasion on the penthouse floor). By the end of January they were meeting almost every day, at first only for an occasional lunch, later at midtown motels. Some weekends, when Benny had business out of town, she would go with him. He never once had accepted her invitation to visit her at home, an apartment in the sixties. He would drop her off in front of the building, watch her enter the vestibule and disappear inside, then wait a few more seconds before driving off. So far, everything had worked out just fine.

But Crissy, predictably, was not entirely happy. He didn't fault her for wanting more. *He* did too. The relationship had grown; sex was only a part of it. The rest could not thrive in motel rooms. They both had come to realize the seriousness of their commitment, and Benny was now ready to take action. Hattie, after all, was ancient history. He didn't wish her ill, but for a long time, even before Crissy came along, he had known that he would leave Hattie some day. Well, the day had come.

Kenneth was the key. His plans for Kenneth had to be unambiguous, clear-cut and convincing . . . .

Next to him, Hattie stirred and mumbled in her sleep. Benny slipped out of bed and went downstairs, carrying his slippers and his bathrobe. He put these on in the kitchen, after closing the door behind him. There was leftover pepper steak in the refrigerator and he helped himself to some, eating it cold — something he could never have done with Hattie around. She would insist on heating it. Afterwards, he drank a beer and reviewed his plan once again.

It was simple really. The easiest part was leaving Hattie with a comfortable income. He would be more than generous. The house would be hers, and anything else she wanted of their belongings. He would be happy to walk away with only a change of clothing. Half of their joint account would go to her, no haggling over that. But the most important part of the plan was to take out a new mortgage on the house — it had been free and clear for over fifteen years now — and give most of the money to his son, so that Kenneth could concentrate on his painting without having to work part time at an art supply store or anywhere else to earn enough to pay his bills. He would keep Hattie as his primary beneficiary on his insurance policies and his pension fund but Kenneth's name would be added on.

The most pressing reason for getting the plan under way was the change he'd noticed in Kenneth. Lately he'd been depressed, at times looked positively ill. When Benny asked him whether he had enough money, if he had caught a cold, if he wanted a loan from his father, his son shook his head and changed the subject. Benny knew that Kenneth's part-time job in an art supply store netted only a few extra dollars a week. Was he hard up for money and too proud to ask?

Well, all that would soon change. His plan would put Kenneth out of Hattie's reach, but, more important, it would free him from financial worries so he could finish some of the canvases stacked against the walls of the loft.

That cluttered world had always reminded Benny of things dying rather than a bright future. Canvases were begun then put aside, sometimes for months. But one day, at lunch, Kenneth had given his father a small parcel. "I did it quickly, just last week," he said, as though to forestall disappointment. "An anniversary present for you and mom. Hope you like it." When Benny started to remove the tape that held the brown wrapping paper, Kenneth stopped him. "No. Open it when you get home. Better still, give it to mom to open."

It was one of the few times Hattie had been reduced to silence. She had stared at the picture in its simple frame for a long time and finally had asked Benny to hang it above the kitchen door. "Is that the best place for it, the kitchen?" Benny had ventured. "Oils can be washed," was her answer. He had put it up, wondering at her choice. He got his answer one morning, when he had come down to breakfast earlier than usual and had found her leaning against the sink, studying the painting with concentration. She had turned away quickly when he appeared in the doorway, but he saw she was embarrassed to have been caught looking at it that way.

It showed Hattie by the sink, preparing supper. Pots, pans, dishes, were on the burners, vegetables on top of the work counter. Hattie was busy peeling potatoes. Benny's face was barely discernible outside the kitchen window, a shadow among other shadows. The picture had had a strange effect on Benny. He realized his son had captured an essential element of their existence. They were indeed, both of them, outsiders looking in.

All that was about to change.

The argument had to be tight, no loose ends.

The big question was: How would Kenneth take the news about Crissy? Kenneth tended to be protective of Hattie, in spite of his mother's constant criticism. Would he side with her against Benny?

Well, every man has to build the road on which he chooses to walk. His road led to a life with Crissy. She was something he desperately needed to retain his manhood, his sanity. Crissy had given him a new purpose. Nothing was too difficult or demanding with Crissy by his side. The difference in their ages — she was thirty-four, Benny fifty-nine — they had agreed, didn't matter. Hattie, of course, would make the most of it to fuel her anger. *A man his age, running after a woman who could be his daughter!* Well, let her rave! It was Kenneth's approval he needed, not hers!

First he would tell Kenneth about the offer in Ohio. The insurance firm had offices there, and Benny's initial inquiries had had positive results. There would be more money too, and that would help, although it wasn't a major consideration. The move to Dayton meant wiping the slate clean, starting a new life with Crissy, new friends, freedom.

Outside a car started, came to a stop at the traffic light at the end of the street, then started up again and moved on. It was the only sound that had intruded all the while he had sat in the kitchen. How long had he been there? Behind him the clock read five-.twenty.

He was in no mood to go back to bed. He shook his head remembering how long it had taken him to convince Hattie they would be more comfortable with separate beds. She'd finally agreed . . . just when he had made up his mind that what they really needed was separate lives . . . .

He rose and began putting out breakfast utensils, The coffee was ready — he had gotten into the habit of setting it up the night before to be sure it was strong, the way he liked it (Hattie skimped on the measurement) — and now he turned on the flame under the pot.

Soon the aroma of fresh coffee filled the kitchen. Benny glanced at the closed door, afraid that the smell would reach Hattie upstairs and bring her down to check things out. He still needed time to think and didn't want her barging in with a barrage of questions. *Why was he up so early? Why hadn't he called her? Why had he made breakfast this morning? Why was he leaving at this time?*

He moved silently and effortlessly, stifling every possible noise, putting dishes down carefully, tiptoeing even though he wore soft slippers. After a second cup of coffee, some orange juice and a slice of toast, he went upstairs to shower. Hattie was still asleep.

When he came out of the bathroom, she was sitting on the edge of the bed, her robe in her hands. She turned to him but said nothing. She was always lethargic in the morning. Benny dressed quickly, while Hattie used the bathroom. By the time she emerged, he was all set to go, his coat over his arm, his briefcase in his hand. He felt foolish standing like that in their bedroom. But today he was especially impatient to get away. He told Hattie he had to review some reports that had to be turned in, later that morning. The gods, mercifully, were on his side. At this hour, Hattie was still heavy-eyed and heavy-souled. He would be spared watching her thawing out, getting ready to shape the day in her image.

Once settled in his office, he called Kenneth and arranged to meet him for lunch at a bistro near New York University. He cleared his desk and told his secretary he was taking the afternoon off for some personal business.

Kenneth looked worse than he had the last time they had met for lunch, about two weeks earlier. Still, he chatted easily with his father through the meal. But over coffee, as Benny described his plan, Kenneth grew restless, impatient even. What Benny had anticipated as an eager response on Kenneth's part turned out to be an obstinate refusal to consider what Benny proposed.

Patiently, Benny retraced his steps, picked up clues that might help him answer Kenneth's objections; moved into awkward silences to rephrase an argument; asked questions in an effort to understand. It soon became painfully clear that, for reasons Kenneth could not or would not express, nothing Benny had put forward was acceptable to him. Finally, his son had said:

"Look, Pa, I know you mean well, and, as far as your own future, I wouldn't dream of stopping you or criticizing you. God knows you've been through a lot with Mom. I know how difficult she is. I'd be the last to say 'Don't do it.' You deserve this chance."

"Well, if you understand that, you understand the rest!" Benny had replied with a touch of asperity.

"I can't leave right now."

"But *why* for heavens sake! You can paint anywhere, you don't have to stay here!" When his son didn't answer, he went on: "If it's Johnnie you're worried about — " His son shook his head.

"No, Johnnie's not the problem. "

"What *is* the problem?" At that point, Benny had paid the bill, and they had walked out toward to the park. They had sat down on a bench, still trying to sound each other out without trespassing on raw emotions. In spite of his obstinate objections, Kenneth was ready to continue the conversation. To Benny, nothing Kenneth said made any sense. He tried to control his mounting frustration.

"Let me get this right," he began again. "You don't want to leave New York right now?"

Kenneth frowned as he nodded. "I guess you could say that, yes."

"When then? When *could* you leave?"

"I'm not sure . . . ."

"For God's sake, Kenneth! This is the chance of a lifetime. What in heaven's name is holding you back? Don't you want to be independent?"

"This is not the time . . . . "

"What do you mean? When did you have in mind?" Benny asked again, and without waiting for his son's reply went on: "All right. So you stay in New York. Fine. We can work it out."

Kenneth shook his head. "Dad, it's not that simple."

"So, tell me. Tell me what's so hard."

"What you're offering me is . . . . " Helplessly, Benny watched his son struggling for control. "Two years ago, last year even, I would have jumped at the chance — "

"What's so different that you can't do it this year, right now? Please Kenneth, help me to understand. I've planned all this with *you* in mind. My own life, Crissy, your mother — everything depends on your taking me up on this! I can't leave without doing this for you. You're my son. I want to help you. I want you to have what would be coming to you sooner or later anyway. Why can't you accept it now? "

He sensed defeat. Choking back disappointment, Benny tried to read Kenneth's expression. For a moment father and son stared at one another, then Kenneth reached out and touched his father's arm. Benny felt himself losing control.

"So tell me. What is it that makes it impossible for you to accept what I'm offering? I can't leave unless you go along with my plan. I won't have any peace knowing that when I'm gone your mother will hound you, wear you down. She may not mean to, but she won't give you a moment's peace." He raised his head in a defiant gesture, challenging his son to contradict him.

"I know all that!!" his son retorted, in a husky voice. Abruptly, he shifted his body to one side, as though to avoid his father's probing look. "Don't you think I want what you're offering?" He turned back just as suddenly. His eyes were bright, feverish. His mouth trembled, as though he was about to burst into tears. It was an expression Benny had not seen for many years, not since his son had come home one day in his gym shorts because the other boys had stolen his trousers and shoes from his locker.

A flash, an elusive intuition made Benny reach out and touch his son. "What's wrong?"

"I'm sick, Dad. I can't go away, not now . . . . I've lost ten pounds since the beginning of the year. And I'm getting weaker . . . ."

He felt a stab of pain, tried to ease his body on the hard bench. For a wild moment, he thought he had died and his soul was struggling to free itself from the bonds of his body. Why else the gasping for breath, this awful numbness in his arms and legs?

Someone was stroking his back. Someone had put an arm around his shoulder, was holding him, cradling him, talking to him. He tried to move away. He needed air, light. His mouth twitched. His eyes would not focus.

"Hey, Dad, c'mon. Don't do this!" he heard his son cry out. Kenneth was hugging him, rocking him gently. Benny let out a deep sigh. "Are you feeling better, Pa?"

"Yes, . . . yes."

"I'm sorry. I'm so sorry!"

"Just give me a a couple of minutes. I felt a bit queasy, that's all." Benny wondered if he would be able to make it back home . . . . No, no, he wasn't going anywhere, not until he'd gotten to the bottom of this. Never had he expected the kind of reaction that now crushed him under the weight of despair. He began again, cautiously:

"I did notice, remember? Last time I saw you? I said you looked thinner. But you said — "

"I didn't want to worry you. "

"You worry me now."

"I'm sorry."

"Well, that's not an answer, is it?" Kenneth sighed. "Let me help you, Kenneth. I can't help you if you keep talking in circles. Just tell me what it is. I'm your father. Do you think I would ever *not* help you?" The look in his son's eyes frightened him.

"Dad, you're the only person I can trust, except for Johnnie. I've always . . . ." His voice trailed off. Benny waited. "You have no idea how many times I tried to tell you, these last six months. I just couldn't. With all the talk, all the publicity, I couldn't bring myself to tell you. Each time I tried, I felt I was dying twice over."

"Dying! Dying! What kind of language is that! So, you're sick. We'll get you better."

"I have AIDS. I've had it for some time."

In the silence that followed, Benny tried desperately to gain his bearings. He sat very still, but his thoughts were in a turmoil. Looking back, he realized the signs had been there all along. Kenneth had definitely lost weight and of late seemed distracted, more withdrawn than usual . . . . Benny berated himself for having missed the obvious, or, rather, for *not* having missed it, and doing nothing about it. But what exactly could he have done? What could he do now? A strange calm settled over him as he realized that it was up to him to start the world turning again.

Get straight answers, for starters. Give his son the kind of reassurance and support he needed. That was the first thing he could do. The second was to shore up their routines, build an emotional levee against the trauma of the news, remain calm while searching out information and examining the choices open to them. No point getting everyone excited or anticipating the worst. After all, new medications were constantly being tested . . . .

Kenneth was hunched over, his head low, his hands clasped in his lap. In as normal a voice as he could muster, Benny said:

"First thing we do is visit your doctor together, just so I can get all the facts . . . ." Benny reached out to his son and touched his arm. "Just tell me what you want." Kenneth kept his head down, his hands clasped in his lap. Benny wondered how other parents, other loved ones reacted to this news. Out loud he said: "Your mother doesn't need to know, not right away. Is that all right?" Kenneth nodded. "Whatever you want, son. Just tell me. Don't worry about me. My plans can wait a bit longer. What's important is you, your future."

His son let out a stifled sob. Benny felt his stomach lurch but went right on. "Listen to me. We can't read what lies ahead, despite what some people say. Meantime, we're very much alive, Kenneth, we're alive until we stop breathing. But if the will collapses, sure, we walk and eat and talk and breathe, but we're more dead than a corpse. Damn it, I'm not letting that happen to either of us." His son remained silent. "The way I see it, the day still has twenty four hours and we've got to fill every single hour of every day."

To Benny it was as though he was talking to his eight-year old again, telling him how the world works, why boys will steal trousers and shoes and force another human being to walk home in gym shorts.

Kenneth raised his head. "I should have told you sooner, I know. I just didn't have the guts!" Benny got up, stretching to his full height as he did so. His son also rose, his hands gripping the edge of the bench as he pushed himself up. He was very pale. Benny had to resist the urge to reach out, touch him.

"Son, you've got plenty of guts, more than I'll ever have." He was rewarded by a thin smile.

"Do I have a choice?"

"Yes, yes, you do. We all have choices until the moment we physically die. It's a matter of adjustment. We're free when we know our limits and make choices within those limits." His son actually grinned.

"You were always good at making us think away our problems."

"No, son, you're wrong about that," replied his father. "I was teaching you to face them."

"Well, I didn't have the guts to do that, did I?"

"But you did. You showed plenty of guts just now. I can tell you something else, too. I'm your father and I've known you a long time. You have plenty of strength to handle this and anything else that comes along. We just need to set down some new rules. We'll do that together, the two of us."

Kenneth patted his father's arm. "Are you sure you want to come with me to my doctor?"

"Of course, I'm sure. Just let me know when."

"All right."

Benny watched his son walk toward Broadway. He didn't move until Kenneth had rounded a corner and was no longer in sight. For a few more seconds he continued to look down the street. He wished he could be invisible, follow his son back to the loft, to his unfinished paintings, to a life that he wanted desperately to trace and fill in and catalog before . . . .

He called Hattie from a nearby bar and told her he had to work later than usual and not to leave any supper for him. Then he ordered a large scotch and tried to sort things out.

With a third scotch he decided Crissy was the only one who should be told, since their plans for moving to Dayton now had to be scrapped. The thought that he might lose her was only a minor ache.

Then, as he sat nursing his drink, the past rushed over him, without warning, a rogue wave, shattering his fragile resolutions. He gripped the edge of the table where he sat, waited for the dizziness to pass. Images rose before him, evenings in their first small house in the upper Bronx, near the zoo, when they would take turns putting the children to bed: the girls in the double-decker set up in a small back room; Kenneth in his tiny cot in a large closet Benny had gutted for him and which remained the boy's "den" until they moved to a larger house. He would listen to their prayers. "Now I lay me down to sleep / and pray the Lord my soul to keep. / If I should die before I wake, / I pray the Lord my soul to take." Somehow Kenneth never got it quite right. Hattie would go over it with him again and again, but it always came out ". . . If I should wake before I die . . . ." Benny had never corrected the boy the way Hattie had tried to do so many times. He didn't have the heart to watch his young son repeat after Hattie, trying so hard to please her, then promptly fall back into his own refrain. To Benny, it didn't matter how the words came out. He nurtured the warm glow that spread inside him when he sat on his son's cot and watched him drift off to sleep. Perfect moments of safe haven, unspoken love. He had never been one to scold. Hattie did enough of that.

Now, he found himself mouthing the little poem, his eyes closed, reaching out for that moment of innocence where a simple prayer could exorcise a boy's night terrors.

"If I should wake before I die . . . ."

Rites of passage are in single file, someone had said to him once, as they snaked around a hotel ballroom at a convention in Georgia. The moment took on an eerie clarity. He could see again the man's face, his bloodshot eyes, his frantic efforts to pack in a good time . . . . It all came back to him, a flood of unrelated memories that somehow had relevance. He found himself thinking: *You die alone and most of the years in between you are alone too.* The desolate look in his son's face told him there was nothing either of them could do to ease the passage.

Back home, he opened the door quietly and went in. He hoped Hattie was asleep.

Tomorrow he would take a long lunch hour and shop for twin beds.

MR. GOLD

From the bay window in her father's study, Kitty peered out through the drawn blinds and waited. She had been standing in that same spot for quite a long time, apprehensive about the possibility of being discovered where she wasn't supposed to be, but unable to pull herself away. She could hear Agnes getting the guest room ready upstairs, running the water in the bathtub to rinse it out. Her mother had gone to the attic after their quick lunch, to sort through the big blue trunk that had once been grandma's, coming back downstairs twice with armloads of scrapbooks which she placed on the coffee table in the living room. Now, she was in the bedroom, washing up. Kitty knew she was still quite safe from being discovered where she should not be; nonetheless, she kept her ears open for any warning sounds.

A tremor of excitement ran through the little girl. She had tiptoed into the study earlier, certain that her mother would not have approved but unable to contain her curiosity about the stranger who was coming to their house, any minute now, someone special, for whom all sorts of preparations had been made. She had stood quietly, unmoving, in that same spot, her large expressive eyes glued to the open gate at the end of their driveway, where the gravel path began its sloping long curve upward, past the study window, before continuing around the corner to the front of the house.

She pushed the blinds further apart to stare in surprise as a cab stopped at the entrance to the driveway instead of continuing up to the front door — another piece of the puzzle that was part of that altogether strange day, one that had begun just after breakfast, with the call her mother had answered and Kitty had overheard.

It was a Mr. Gold. He had flown in two days ago and would be coming to see them that afternoon.

The man who walked up the driveway slowly, at a slight angle to compensate for the incline of the ground, gazed at the pebbles of the roadway as though searching for the proper place for his feet. His overcoat was open and he wore no hat, as though celebrating the new Spring that had moved in stealthily, over the past few days, out of a lingering winter chill. Once he paused and looked up at the house. Kitty drew back instinctively, but there was no reason to do so. Mr. Gold could not possibly see her peering out between the drawn blinds. Once, he looked behind him, back along the driveway, before resuming his slow walk, past the study window, around to the front of the house.

When the bell rang, Kitty ran into the foyer and opened the door. Mr. Gold stared at Kitty then looked past her, over her head, into the large entrance foyer, up the winding stairs. He seemed disoriented, nervous. Without moving, he gave Kitty the impression of sudden wariness and betrayed a subdued excitement that communicated itself to her and kept her rooted to the spot. She continued to stare at him as she stood by the side of the open door. She was a big girl for her age, taller than most of her friends and classmates, and surprisingly mature for her age. Those who did not know her, treated her as a teenager at first; but she was only eight years old and just a child.

Her mother came floating down the stairs, patting down her hair. She looked fresh and clean and lovely. "Why, Mr. Gold! You're early!" She went up to the stranger and took his coat. "Do come inside . . . . Don't just stand

there, Kitty! Close the door . . . . " She hung the stranger's
coat inside the hall closet and took his arm. "Agnes must
still be upstairs. I'm sorry. I heard the bell, but I was
finishing dressing," she said pleasantly to Mr. Gold; and to
Kitty, over her shoulder as she led the visitor through the
foyer toward the living room: "Tell Agnes to make tea and
bring it in." She stood aside as Mr. Gold entered the living
room, then looked back to Kitty who had not moved and
waved her away with a touch of impatience. "Go on, go on.
Tell Agnes to make tea!" The door closed softly behind
her. Kitty remained standing for a moment, then sat down
in the big oak chair that stood by the entrance, next to the
umbrella rack and the coat closet. She wondered why Mr.
Gold didn't greet her, why her mother didn't put her arm
around her and say something nice as she always did when
friends came to visit.

Agnes found her there when she came downstairs.
Obviously she had not heard the bell. "For goodnesssake!
Why are you sitting there?" The thin sound of voices from
behind the closed door of the living room reached them.
"He's here already?" Kitty nodded.

"Mama wants you to make tea and bring it in."

Agnes nodded and went on down the hall, past the
stairs, into the kitchen. Ordinarily Kitty would have trailed
behind. She loved to be with Agnes. Agnes was always
willing to be interrupted, would always talk to her; Kitty
couldn't remember a time without Agnes. Her mother had
told her once that she was Daddy's cousin third removed,
whatever that was. Her mother had tried to explain, but
Kitty had not really understood. Anyway, it didn't matter.
She loved Agnes, almost as much as she loved her mother
and Daddy. She was kind and pleasant, and fun to be with.
But today, as she heard the sound of cups and saucers
being taken out of the cupboard, the faucet turned on, the
pot filled for tea, Kitty was irresistibly drawn in the other

direction, to the closed door of the living room. She could barely make out the voices, but suddenly her mother's words reached her, clear as a bell:

" — the Melzers, they spent a weekend with her parents, they were friends of mom's, remember? On that Sunday afternoon, they rushed off home for what they called their ablutions." Her mother's giggled. "Oh, and here's Sam Brody, you remember Sam, don't you George? He always had wet hair. I don't know why." There was a murmur from George. "Ah, here's the one I've been looking for! Here *you* are, George! You and Elliott in that godawful getup you managed for the New Year's eve charity ball." There was a small pause. "Yes, that was the year . . . ." Mr. Gold must have said something unpleasant because Kitty heard her mother utter a shrill little cry and her voice, when she replied, had a high unnatural tone. "That's right. Nine years ago this last New Year's . . . . You won't forget what you promised me, George! Not a word, about that. Not even here, not even when we're alone! Not with me, not with Elliott, not with anyone! It was my one and only condition, remember? You agreed!" Mr. Gold said something in a soothing, voice, but Kitty could not make out the words. Instead she heard her mother say: "Of course not. Nothing of the sort. I wouldn't hear of your going off again, George. After all, you're family!"

The kitchen had become quiet again. Kitty tiptoed from the door and went upstairs to her room. She was not a devious girl, not at all suspicious or given to spying or disobedience, but the events of that morning had not quite settled inside her. She was curious about the visitor, who he was and what had brought him there. But even without immediate answers to the questions that crowded her perception of what was happening, she sensed, with that infallible instinct that children have at a certain age, that Mr. Gold's coming had already changed their lives, just how she couldn't explain, but she recognized the signs of upheaval and mystery.

In her room she sat down and tried to sort out the impressions that flashed before her and dazzled her into a state of confusion. After a while she heard Agnes moving down the front hall with the tea tray, resting it on the small table beside the door in order to knock. Her mother came to the door, said something to Agnes, and took in the tray. Kitty heard the door close again and Agnes's footsteps as she walked back to the kitchen. She could make out the familiar sound of dishes being put away, the refrigerator door opening and closing.

Mr. Gold. George. He was family, her mother had said. But the only family Kitty knew was Daddy's brother, Uncle David, who lived with his wife Helen and her cousins Tommy and Sara in New York, and all of them had the same name she had, and Daddy's sister Genny, who was divorced from Bobby Stern and now lived in Los Angeles where she worked for Warner Brothers. Daddy had told her all about the different names a long time ago and that Mommy's name, before she married Daddy, had been De Lourian. She had learned to spell it too, because it was part of her name as well: Katherine De Lourian Callahan. So how could Mr. Gold be family?

She was still sitting in her chair when she heard Agnes on the stairs. Quickly Kitty picked up a book from the top of the dresser and opened it as Agnes came into the room carrying her afternoon snack. "You forgot all about my luscious double chocolate cake. How come?" She watched Kitty put down the book and take the tray into her lap. "Are you feeling all right?" she went on in a different tone, studying Kitty under a slight frown. She put a hand on Kitty's forehead. "Let's not have you coming down with something! Not today, please, God?" She watched as Kitty drank some milk and took a large bite of cake.

"Mr. Gold —" Kitty began, not at all sure what she wanted to say.

"Mr. Gold!" Agnes laughed and Kitty smiled at the familiar pleasant sound. "Never mind Mr. Gold," she went on, picking up some crumbs that had fallen on Kitty's dress. "How can you think of anything besides this luscious cake you've been waiting for all day?"

Kitty took a large bite of the cake. She drank from the tall glass of milk. Agnes stood by watching.

"Well? How is it?" Kitty nodded vigorously, her mouth full. "That's better," said Agnes, visibly relieved. She turned to leave, then came back to where Kitty sat and peered down into her face. "Are you sure you're all right?"

"I'm fine, honest."

She finished the cake — it was very good, but then Agnes never made anything that wasn't good — and put the tray down on the dresser. She moved to the window where the trim lawn spread out beyond the shadow of the house, ending at the edge of a thick glade that bordered on to the next property. When Kitty was younger, her mother used to make up stories for her about fairies and magic birds who lived in that small wooded patch. Kitty could still remember her first reaction, hearing about those invisible denizens of their back yard — a mixture of excitement and a touch of fear. She still carried the details in her memory, but she had come to look upon the stories and the storytelling as part of a past belonging to a very little girl who was no longer there, who was now some other Kitty she was just beginning to know, just starting to feel comfortable with.

She was startled by her mother's voice from the patio just under her window. Bending down to peek out, she saw her mother and Mr. Gold sitting in the big cane chairs with the striped blue cushions. They had taken their tea cups with them. Her mother was saying. "You'll have plenty of time to settle in, George. Elliott is coming back early today. He'll be here any minute, in fact. He said he'd drive back with you to the station to pick up your bags. Then, tomorrow he'll take you to look at the places he's found for you."

"Are you sure you . . . you want me here, so close? It's not too late, Mary — "

Her mother's voice was clipped and sure. "What nonsense. You're family, George! Why shouldn't you be close by, especially now that Rose is gone and you're all alone?"

"You have no idea how often I've thought about . . . no, *relived* that time, wondering —" He was interrupted by her mother, who had put down her cup as he spoke and walked to the edge of the patio. She stood there, her arms crossed tightly across her chest, staring at the expanse of struggling new lawn in front of her. After a few seconds she turned and said, in an unfamiliar harsh voice: "You do understand, don't you, George? I told you, I don't want to dredge up any of it. That part of our lives must remain buried."

George lowered his head and nodded. "It's just that I've never been able to forgive myself — bringing him into the house, Mom and everybody being so nice to him, his promises, his glib talk. Oh, God, Mary, every time I think back . . . ." His voice trailed off and when he spoke again it was so low that Kitty couldn't hear what he said. Her mother shook her head impatiently and looked away again.

"Not you. Me. *I* was the naive one, the stupid one. So you can stop blaming yourself, George." She gave a little laugh, almost a stifled sob. "After all, it happens every day, somewhere, to some young girl who dreams about — " Her voice trailed off in a wide gesture that encompassed the entire patio, the house, the world. Kitty instinctively drew close to the wall, as though her mother's pain had for a moment reached inside her, too. For her mother was suffering. Kitty could tell from the way she held her body, from the sound of her voice, thin and threatening to snap. When she spoke again the words were flat and colorless.

She had come back to sit in her chair and now leaned over and touched Mr. Gold's arm. "I do want you here, George. You musn't doubt that for a single moment. But you've got to help me. All of that is over and done with. I don't want to leaf through those pages ever again. Please . . . ." Mr. Gold nodded and patted the hand that rested on his arm.

"Yes, yes, of course. It's just that coming here, seeing you, seeing Kitty —" Her mother pulled back, as though struck.

"Leave Kitty out of it. Especially Kitty! Not a sound, not a look. Do you understand?" Then, in a steadier voice, as though reciting a lesson: "I haven't told her anything yet. We'll explain later who you are, why she doesn't remember you, that you've been far away for all this time."

Mr. Gold shifted in his seat. Now he picked up his teacup and took a sip. Kitty could hear the cup rattle against the saucer. After a while, her mother took the cup from him and set it down on the table next to her. "I know how you feel, why you left so suddenly and never wrote. But like I told you on the phone when you first called, George, I've settled the account in my book. The past is closed. There are no hopes to be shattered again, nothing to mourn. I am alive. I have Kitty. You are family and belong here. That's the whole of it." There was a pause and then Mr. Gold said:

"When Rose died, I just quit on everything and everybody. I sold the house in less than two weeks. I don't know how your letter caught up with me in Hong Kong, that's fate for you. Anyway, I'm glad it did, and I'm glad I'm here. You were very kind, Mary. I didn't realize until you wrote how much I had missed you and Mom, how lonely I was . . . ."

"Hong Kong, of all places! When Elliott tracked you down through Rose's obituary in the *Times*, we agreed we should try to get you back home. I never expected to get an answer to my letter." There was a brief silence. "I just couldn't see you living out the rest of your life alone like that, George. We missed you, too. Mom never let on much, but I could tell she would have given anything to see you again. But I couldn't bring myself to do much then. Not until now. I never blamed you, but I just couldn't face the past yet. Then I realized we'll always be carrying those ghosts inside us, wherever we happen to be. And I wanted so badly to see you again, talk to you. . . . . I wish I'd realized it while Mom was still alive. She missed you so much . . . . If your father had lived, if Hugh had been around, he might have helped her through the bad times. But there was no one. I certainly wasn't there for her. And your going off like that . . . . We both understood, we just couldn't talk about it. That's why I think she probably suffered the most, you know? She never said anything, for my sake and yours. She loved both of us too much. And she missed your father. Hugh had been very kind to us. I scarcely remember my own dad. Hugh had given me a real home. I always thought of him as my real dad. Then you came along. We had a lot of good years growing up . . . . I think Mom knew that if we could live out that terrible time after Hugh died, after . . . what happened," there was a pause during which her mother cleared her throat — "there might be something to salvage eventually. She never blamed me for being silly and stupid in my infatuation, or you for having brought him here then going off abruptly, not writing — " After a while she relaxed in her chair, her arms loose in her lap, her head resting against the striped cushion behind her. "It was an awful time for the two of us.

Your father dead, you out there somewhere . . . . ." She stifled a small cry and sat forward suddenly, clasping her hands in her lap, her head lowered.

Mr. Gold placed a hand on her folded ones. Kitty winced. Who was he to touch her mother like that! Was he really family? Even Uncle David didn't do things like that. But then, this was a conversation unlike any Kitty had ever heard. Mr. Gold was saying something, almost whispering. All Kitty heard was: ". . . how much I hated myself, hated *him*, how I rejoiced when I heard he had been killed in an automobile crash." Her mother's small voice floated up to her. "I never hated him, George, never. I wanted to die, but that was *my* weakness."

George patted her hands again and drew himself up in the chair. "I suppose it had to come around full circle. All things do eventually."

"I'm not sure, but yes, it did, didn't it? With us, I mean? I've often wondered —"

A sound made Kitty turn toward the door. Agnes! She ran to the bed and lay down on it, closing her eyes. When Agnes came in, Kitty was stretched out as though she had been dozing.

"Are you sure you're all right, Kitty?"

She tried to looked startled, not realizing how successfully she was responding to an innate urgency that forced her to dissemble, reacting to the fear that had sprung unbidden full-blown inside her at that moment when she had felt the instinctive need to camouflage her confusion and uncertainties. Something inside her told her she could not share any of her feelings with anyone, not even Agnes. In that brief moment, all of that washed across her consciousness like a huge wave that carried her back to shore. She did not then understand that she had stumbled on her own future, turning the corner forever on one large vista of her untroubled childhood. Years later, she would remember that day with confused but vivid memories, the soft April afternoon, the thin sunlight slanted across the patio, the curtains moving lazily in the small breeze, all part of a scene etched in her vision for all time. But at that moment, all she knew was that she had to withdraw from the kind eyes of those who were there to protect her, those who loved her — Agnes, her mother, Daddy, yes, even Mr. Gold, about whom she knew nothing except that she must accept him since her mother seemed to have done so. A secret had tumbled into the middle of her day, a secret she knew she must not give away. Without grasping why it should be so, she knew no one could help her find her way out of the dark dusty corner she had stumbled into on this mild April afternoon, an afternoon unlike any she had ever known. The certainty that she must be cautious, maintain her distance, prompted the wide careless gesture, the stifled yawn, as she turned toward Agnes.

"I guess I dozed off." Then, as Agnes moved to pick up the tray, she remembered to add, with wide eyes: "The cake was yummy!"

She had succeeded in distracting Agnes, who gave her a fond smile. "Well, I guess you can't be too sick if you ate that big piece!"

She followed Agnes out of the room and watched her start down the stairs, one step at a time, as she planted one foot firmly next to the other before going on, a familiar routine. Kitty, as usual, kept a certain distance, giving Agnes space to negotiate the descent into the front hall while balancing the tray high in the air.

"Now, Kitty, remember, you musn't — " but Agnes's words were left forever hanging on the stairs, for just then they all heard the car as it shifted gears and raced up the long sloping drive to the front of the house. Kitty rushed down past Agnes, almost tripping her. She swung the front door open, as her mother and Mr. Gold came around from the patio. They too had heard the car. For a moment Kitty's eyes locked into her mother's, those deep blue pools that had always been a source of wonder and joy to her. They were so different from her own hazel eyes and her father's large soft dark brown ones. For one brief eternity she saw her own uncertainties reflected in them, a touch of fear even. It was gone just as quickly.

As Kitty rushed past, her mother frowned and turned to Agnes, who had put down the tray on the hall table and was now standing in the doorway.

"What has she been up to?"

"She was dozing upstairs, Mary."

The car had come to a stop. Her mother moved toward it, Mr. Gold by her side; but Kitty was already there, tugging at the driver's door.

"Daddy! You're home early!"

He laughed, bending to kiss her. Kitty buried her head into his neck, peering around at her mother who stood waiting, at Mr. Gold standing to one side, at Agnes smiling in the doorway. She smelled her father's tweeds, his after-shave lotion. His arms were strong and familiar around her. When he finally pulled back and stood up, Kitty struggled to hold on to him a bit longer. He studied her face for a few seconds, then asked:

"And what are *you* doing home so early?"

Her mother replied for her: "Mrs. Stanton came down with something. They dismissed the children before lunch today." Her father smiled down at her.

"Why aren't you playing with Sandy, then?"

"She's coming in a little while, with her new robots game," said Kitty. "She had to go to the Mall first, with her Mom, to get new sneakers. I had a nap and ate Agnes's chocolate cake."

"Not all of it!" Kitty giggled and shook her head. "Oh, well, that's all right then —" said her father, patting her head. He turned to Mr. Gold. "Well, George, it's been a long time!" The men shook hands.

Perhaps it was her father's reassuring presence that made her forget her earlier curiosity. She followed Agnes into the kitchen, no longer wanting to hear anything the grownups said to one another.

She stood watching Agnes peeling carrots at the sink. Agnes scowled down at her, but she was smiling. "Go on," said Agnes. "Go out and play. Sandy will be here any minute now."

She ran down the long corridor into the soft pale April afternoon. The patio, the lawn, the glade behind it were once more a familiar place, safe and friendly. She went into the shed that her father had cleared out for her, where she brought her friends and stored her toys. The new bike shone in the half-light and she marveled again at it, her parents' Christmas gift. She had learned quickly to balance herself and to negotiate turns and brake easily, but she had promised not to ride alone until Daddy said it was all right. Now she settled on the seat, held on to the handlebars as though about to take off. She knew the bike had accepted her, would not betray her. Soon she would be able to ride down the street, maybe even as far as the Mall.

THE CRITICS

["Buried Treasure," in *Sepia Tones*] "The jewel in [the final] section — indeed the masterpiece of the entire anthology — is Anne Paolucci's 'Buried Treasure,' a brilliant, haunting memoir of an unforgettable Italian American man narrated by his daughter-in-law."
Review of *The Voices We Carry* in *The Women's Review of Books,* July 1994.

["The Oracle is Dumb or Cheat," in *Sepia Tones*] "The rambling narrative is written as if learned secondhand, the narrator's voice yet another gossip . . . . By the end of the book, the author has invoked the world of an ingrown community where family pride cautions, 'Keep your eyes shut and say nothing . . . . Dust always settles.' "
Review in the *New York Times,* February 1986.

[*Sepia Tones*] "These seven short stories, beautifully written and utterly absorbing, are the work of a genuinely literary artist. The author's insight into her various characters is of such clairvoyance as to make them universal. Anne Paolucci combines qualities seldom found in the same writer: a sure sense of narrative, a marked talent for writing effective dialogue, and a distinctive style that constantly engages the reader with its warmth. *Sepia Tones* should bring its author the recognition she merits as an important American writer. I cannot imagine any discriminating reader experiencing the pleasure of reading these stories without wanting to read more of the author's writings."
Jerre Mangione, Writer

[*Sepia Tones*] "Una strana tensione accomuna tutti I personaggi di questi racconti, quella che non si ferma all'apparenza, quella che scava nel proprio animo alla ricerca di nuove ragioni per vivere, quella che non si accontenta di restarsene ferma ma sogna nuovi cieli nuovi paesi nuove certezze economiche, quella che rende simili in fondo tutti gli emigranti, e ne sottolinea l'ansia i dubbi e le abitudini ataviche i vizi dell'antico vicinato trasportati nel nuovo . . . . Una lezione eroica di vita, e anche un'occasione per sentire tutta l'aderenza ad una doppia cultura, la coscienza chiara di appartenere contemporaneamente a due mondi, all'apparenza lontani, ma che finiscono invece il ritrovarsi vicini e quasi coincidere."
Review in *Due Mondi,* January 1986

[*Sepia Tones*] "Her earlier stories covered a wide spectrum of situations and a rich variety of people, drawn from different

social and economic backgrounds. *Sepia Tones* focuses on the rich Italian-American ethnic experience in its multi-faceted reality. The reminiscences of "A Small Clearing," and "Don Giacomo" are different in their emotional coloring from "Buried Treasure" — a story which is tender and funny at the same time. "The Oracle is Dumb or Cheat" is a stylistic tour-de-force in its musical effects and its powerful refrain. "Ciao, mio tesoro," records the painful loss of a young husband and father, told from the point of view of the widow. "Rarà" and "Lights" are clearly related to the others but not in any obvious way. The characters of one appear in one or more of the other stories, but there is no effort to force connections . . . . The reader can identify easily with both the people and the situations."

Review in The Italian Voice, 1986.

[*Sepia Tones*] "A fine collection of stories, which is also a superb chronicle of shifting ethnic values in the American setting . . . . "

Nishan Parlakian, Playwright